A note on BLACKWATER

Michael McDowell has taken on a
remarkable challenge with a novel the scope
of BLACKWATER.

His work has ranged from the contemporary
novel of horror set in the American South
(THE AMULET, COLD MOON OVER
BABYLON, and THE ELEMENTALS) to the
extravagantly detailed novel of America in
another time (GILDED NEEDLES and
KATIE).

His fullest powers are mustered now in his
six-part novel BLACKWATER, which Peter
Straub, author of GHOST STORY, says
"looks like Michael McDowell's best yet...it
seduces and intrigues...makes us impatient
for the next volume." Straub says McDowell
is "beyond any trace of doubt, one of the
absolutely best writers of horror"; Stephen
King calls McDowell "the finest writer of
paperback originals in America"; and the
Washington Post promises "Cliffhangers
guaranteed."

Avon Books are available at special quantity discounts for bulk purchases for sales promotions, premiums, fund raising or educational use. Special books, or book excerpts, can also be created to fit specific needs.

For details write or telephone the office of the Director of Special Markets, Avon Books, 959 8th Avenue, New York, New York 10019, 212-262-3361.

MICHAEL McDOWELL'S

BLACKWATER: VI

RAIN

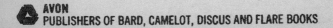

AVON
PUBLISHERS OF BARD, CAMELOT, DISCUS AND FLARE BOOKS

BLACKWATER: VI RAIN is an original publication of Avon Books.
This work has never before appeared in book form.

AVON BOOKS
A division of
The Hearst Corporation
959 Eighth Avenue
New York, New York 10019

Cover illustration by Wayne D. Barlowe

First Avon Printing, June, 1983

Our story 'til now...

In THE FORTUNE, Volume V of the BLACK-WATER saga, the Caskey clan becomes the leading family of Perdido, millionaires many times over. Elinor's mysterious foreknowledge of the existence of oil on swampland held by the family is confirmed by geologists—another proof of her uncanny kinship with the watery world—and she and daughter Miriam lead the family into a period of unparalleled wealth.

Frances—Elinor's second, and favored, daughter—discovers to her alarm that she is pregnant. Though Elinor tries to reassure her about the strange differences that set them apart from the rest of the family, nothing can adequately prepare Frances for the horrors of the childbirth bed. As Elinor had predicted, twins are born: one, named Lilah, who will be greeted with joy by the rest of the family; the other, Nerita, Frances's "river daughter," whose existence must remain a secret from all and who will eventually lure her mother away.

Meanwhile, Sister Haskew, sister of Elinor's husband Oscar, wills herself into invalidism to prevent the return of her husband, Early; Queenie Strickland's long-lost son Malcolm, who had left town in disgrace many years before, is discovered in a small-town barbecue joint by Miriam, and dragged home to rejoin the family; and, in a horrifying resumption of a pattern of inexplicable deaths by drowning, the town of Perdido again loses one of its young to the river.

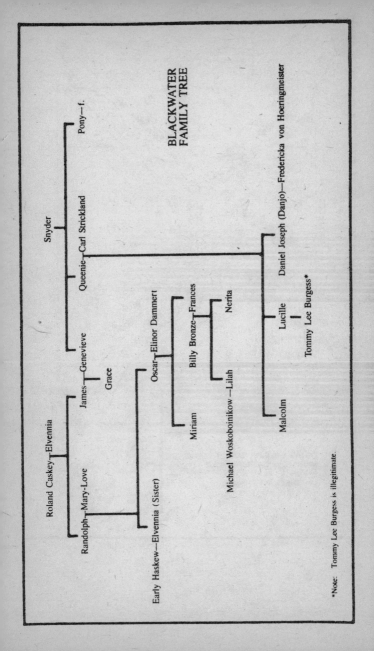

BLACKWATER
FAMILY TREE

Snyder

Pony—f.

Queenie—Carl Strickland

James—Genevieve

Grace

Roland Caskey—Elvennia

Randolph—Mary-Love

Early Haskew—Elvennia (Sister)

Oscar—Elinor Dammert

Miriam

Billy Bronze—Frances

Nerita

Lilah

Michael Woskoboinikow—Lilah

Malcolm

Lucille

Daniel Joseph (Danjo)—Fredericka von Hoeringmeister

Tommy Lee Burgess*

*Note: Tommy Lee Burgess is illegitimate.

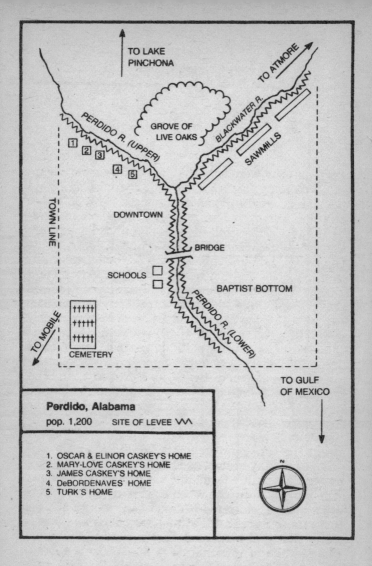

TO LAKE
PINCHONA

TO ATMORE

PERDIDO R. (UPPER)

BLACKWATER R.

GROVE OF
LIVE OAKS

SAWMILLS

① ② ③
④ ⑤

TOWN LINE

DOWNTOWN

BRIDGE

SCHOOLS

BAPTIST BOTTOM

TO MOBILE

PERDIDO R. (LOWER)

†††††
†††††
†††††
CEMETERY

TO GULF
OF MEXICO

N

Perdido, Alabama

pop. 1,200   SITE OF LEVEE 〰️

1. OSCAR & ELINOR CASKEY'S HOME
2. MARY-LOVE CASKEY'S HOME
3. JAMES CASKEY'S HOME
4. DeBORDENAVES' HOME
5. TURK'S HOME

CHAPTER 72

The Engagement

Perhaps they were only that: two old women gossiping, gossiping forever in a back bedroom of an old house in a remote corner of Alabama. In 1958 Sister Haskew was sixty-four-years-old, crippled, bed-ridden, querulous, weak, dependent, and demanding. Queenie Strickland was sixty-six, fat, happy, bustling, devoted, and cheerful. Both women were immensely rich, and neither one of them ever gave a second thought to the money they possessed. Queenie was Sister's slave and spy. Queenie fetched and carried. Queenie left her own house, next door, promptly at six fifty-five in order to bring Sister's breakfast tray to her at seven o'clock every morning, and at seven o'clock every evening, Queenie carried Sister's supper tray down to Ivey's darkened kitchen, and dropped the dishes on the counter with a clatter and a sigh. Sister would never have allowed Queenie away from her beside at all had it not been for Sister's insatiable curiosity about the goings-on of the town, the mill, and her own family. Queenie was allowed to play bridge, go shopping, drive out to her daughter Lucille's farm, and eat dinner next door at Elinor's, only because when she returned to Sister's musty, close, cluttered bedroom, she would be able to relate to Sister all that had been done and everything that had been said. Sister would take these random bits of information and draw wild conclusions and predictions, and invariably Queenie said, "Sister, you are wrong, that's not gone happen." And indeed, Sister's predictions never did come true, not

9

a single one of them. Sister had been so long removed from society that she had almost forgot how it worked. Queenie was a faithful reporter, but Sister's analysis was never correct.

The house in which Sister and Miriam lived had altered its whole character in the past dozen years. When Mary-Love was alive, and during Miriam's adolescence, the place had seemed suffused with a kind of vitality bred—some would say—of meanness, but perhaps really only of energetic purpose. It had firmly stood its ground between Elinor's much larger residence on one side, and James Caskey's more genteel home on the other. Now something in its aspect, with the porches and all the first-floor windows hidden behind azaleas and camellias that had been allowed to grow unchecked, suggested that the house was drawing in upon itself, that it no longer set itself up in any sort of competition with its neighbors, that it wished to retire from the fray. Inside it smelled of age. The furniture was still exactly as it had been on the day of Mary-Love Caskey's death twenty-two years before. This was not out of reverence for the dead woman, but because for one thing Miriam didn't care enough to want to change it, and for another, Sister liked to be reminded as often as possible—although she would never admit it, even to herself—that Mary-Love was, after all, dead. Ivey Sapp was an old woman, too, as old as Queenie, and she had buried Bray in the spring of 1957. She now had Melva, a granddaughter of James's cook, Roxie, to help her. Ivey was fatter even than Queenie, and did nothing but sit in the kitchen all day listening to the radio and giving directions to Melva; she would bestir herself only to cook the few dishes that Sister would eat.

Sister had lain so many years in bed that the entire house smelled of her and her infirmity, a pale powdery lavender sweetness like the herbs used by the Egyptians to fill the cavity of an eviscerated corpse. A person of delicate temperament might have

10

gone mad in that place without ever realizing why. Miriam Caskey, thirty-seven now, was of a temperament robust enough to withstand the fragility of the atmosphere in which she slept every night, though perhaps the air in her room, the door of which she made sure was kept carefully shut all day, was not so sickly.

Though Early Haskew had never returned for Sister, she declared that she could not rest comfortably at night until Miriam had double-checked the locks on all the downstairs doors and windows. "That man will climb through to get at me," Sister constantly declaimed. "That man will raise ladders against the side of the house and peer at me through the window." Miriam had given up arguing that Early, wherever he was, was sixty-four years old, probably very fat, and unlikely to be inclined toward feats of athletic prowess.

Sister and Miriam weren't close. Miriam could not forget that Sister's infirmity, though real enough now, had begun in fakery. After her fall down the stairs, occasioned by her temporary blindness, Sister had taken to bed on account of a supposed weakness in her legs. And in order to avoid her husband, she had kept to that bed, willing her legs to wither so that Early would never have the opportunity to spirit her away from her cherished home. Miriam could not bring herself to cater to a woman who had deliberately crippled herself. And Sister, for her part, felt that Miriam spent too much time with the mill and the Caskey oil business and not enough time with her. Sister said to Queenie, "I'm rich, you know that? I've got so much money I don't have the first idea what to do with it. And you know who it's going to? Every penny goes to Miriam. I've told her so. And how does Miriam treat me? She treats me like I'm a poor cousin."

"I used to be a poor cousin," Queenie pointed out.

"Exactly," said Sister, nodding her head, "and Miriam treats me the way that Mama and everybody else in the family used to treat you. Like I was a no-class, no-account sponger."

This speech startled Queenie, not because it was rude—which it certainly was—but rather because it sounded very much like something Mary-Love Caskey herself might have said. It set Queenie to thinking, and she told herself that she would pay more attention to Sister's manner in the future. Queenie watched, and Queenie listened, and Queenie concluded that Sister was growing more and more like her dead mother.

One day after church, in early fall of 1958, Queenie stopped Miriam outside in the yard, and said, "Miriam, have you noticed something about Sister?"

"You mean that she gets more demanding every day?" The Alabama summer still lingered, and Miriam stripped off her gloves with relief. She unpinned her hat, and shook out her hair.

"No," said Queenie with a little frown. "I mean the fact that she's getting more and more like Mary-Love every day."

Miriam smiled. "Haven't you realized before this? Haven't you seen the way she signs checks?"

"'Elvennia Haskew.' How else would she sign checks?" Queenie returned, surprised.

"No," said Miriam. She turned and went up the steps onto the porch and sat down in a wicker rocker; Queenie did the same. "About a year ago," Miriam continued, "I got called down to the bank because they said somebody was forging Sister's checks. So I went down there, and looked at the checks that had come in. There was 'Elvennia Haskew' all right—but it was in Grandmama's handwriting." Miriam laughed. "My heart jumped, and I thought, 'Lord God, she's come back from the grave, and what are we gone do?' The n's were the same, and the a at the end of the word. Just like Grandmama's. I came back here, and I said, 'Sister, why are you playing games with your signature? You are upsetting the people down at the bank.' And Sister didn't even know what

12

I was talking about. So I showed her her old signature, and then I showed her the one she had just put on that check, and she said, 'I don't see any difference.' I didn't say anything else. But you look sometime, get her to write something out for you—the handwriting is Grandmama's, stroke for stroke."

"You loved your grandmama," remarked Queenie, though the spirit of Miriam's remarks had suggested otherwise.

"I did," said Miriam. "I loved her very, very much. I've never loved anybody as much as I loved her. But thank God she's dead, and thank God she's never coming back. She ruled the roost back then. And right now I rule the roost. So it's just as well that she and I don't have to fight it out."

"If Mary-Love were alive," said Queenie, "she wouldn't be fighting with you. She'd still be fighting with Elinor. She'd leave you alone."

"Nope," said Miriam. "She'd think I was uppity, and she'd try to keep me down. Just like Sister is now. Sister thinks I'm uppity, running the mill the way I do. Never mind that I'm making money for all of us, I'm not paying enough attention to *her*. Not waiting on her hand and foot the way you do."

"I don't mind," said Queenie.

"I know you don't, but I would. And I'd never do it, either. Sister brought all this on herself, Queenie, you know she did. Sister fell down the stairs eleven years ago. She could have been up and around in a few weeks, but all these years later she is still making people wait on her, people that have better things to do with their lives. I love Sister. I was brought up to love Sister. I will love her until the minute she sinks down dead in those five feather mattresses and those seven damned pillows. But I'm never gone say, 'Sister, I'm sorry you're crippled,' or 'Sister, I'm sorry you're lonely up here.' And she knows better than to ask me."

Just then Lilah wandered over from the next door.

Miriam smiled and held out her hands to her eleven-year-old niece. Lilah came up the steps.

"Grandmama says dinner will be ready in fifteen minutes and come on over when you want."

Queenie, whose appetite had never faltered in all her gathering years, stood up immediately. "Coming?" she asked Miriam.

Lilah said quickly, "Miriam, will you take me upstairs and let me see your jewelry?"

"I'll show you some," said Miriam. "And I'll let you try on a few things, too." So Miriam and Lilah went into the house and Queenie walked across the sandy yard to Elinor's, hoping to find something to nibble in the kitchen before they all sat down.

"Who's that?" cried Sister, hearing the sound of footsteps coming up the stairs.

"It's me!" called Miriam. "And Lilah!"

"Lilah, come speak to me!"

Lilah ran down the hall, leaned into Sister's room, and impatiently cried, "Not yet! Miriam's gone let me try on some of her jewelry."

"You try it on and then you come down here and show it to me."

Lilah hurried back to Miriam's room. She feared she had missed what for her was the best part, the opening of the drawer, but she hadn't. Miriam just stood before the dresser, smiling. "I'll let you do it today," she said to Lilah.

Lilah dropped to her knees and reverently pulled out the bottom drawer of the old dresser. In it were stacked nine jewelry boxes, each one of a different size, each of a different age, each of a different texture. To Lilah, they were as dissimilar as any nine persons waiting in line at the bank. And each one was filled with treasure.

"Which one do you want to look in?" asked Miriam.

Lilah pointed to the middle box in the right-hand stack. "This one," she said.

Miriam took a small key from her pocket, and went to a peculiar little chest in the corner of the room. It was as tall as she and as narrow, and had a mirror on the door. Lilah loved this upright chest, for she had never seen one that was anything like it. Inside were a dozen narrow shelves, and on those shelves Miriam kept things no one else was allowed to see. On the top shelf were nothing but keys, hundreds and hundreds of keys that opened God and Miriam only knew what locks. Without hesitation Miriam withdrew a ring of tiny keys from the back, and unerringly inserted one into the lock of the chest that Lilah had chosen. The case opened instantly.

Inside were earrings, jumbled together: bobs in emeralds and bobs in rubies and diamonds; pearl drops in gold settings; tiny golden studs delicately fashioned in the shape of stars, and ships, and horses; fancy antique drops, the like of which Lilah had never known existed, massive with filigreed metalwork and a variety of stones; chaste modern work of single black pearls. Pressing her hands into the box, she was stung with sharp clasps and pins and facets— but she felt a thrill to such pain. It seemed impossible that each piece she picked up had its mate some- where in the welter of gems, but Miriam assured her that it was so. "I don't buy single pieces," Miriam said, "and I never lose anything, so they're all there somewhere."

"Don't you want me to match them up for you?"

"Why bother?" asked Miriam. "We'd just put them right back in the box and they'd all get mixed to- gether again. Besides, Queenie's probably about to starve to death. Pick out a pair and try them on."

Lilah's ears weren't pierced, so she had to find bobs. She found one of a square-cut massive red stone. "What is this?"

"Rhodolite. It's from South Africa. I bought those on Fifth Avenue in New York in 1953."

Miriam thrust her hand into the box, and in an- other second she was holding its mate. Lilah wasn't

15

even certain that Miriam had looked. She seemed to have found it by its *feel*. Miriam clapped the bobs on her niece's ears. They were absurdly heavy, and dragged at the child's lobes.

"How do they look?" cried Lilah, peering into the mirror.

"Very silly," said Miriam. "Now go show Sister— and hurry! My stomach was growling all the way through the sermon this morning."

"I know," said Lilah, scampering out of the door. "I heard it."

Lilah ran down the hall again and entered Sister's room. She went up to Sister's bedside and turned her head this way and that for the jewels to be admired.

"They are precious," said Sister, "and so are you, darling."

"Thank you."

"Miriam never lets anybody but you try on her jewelry."

"She's got so much!" whispered Lilah.

"It's a wonder we can afford to eat in this house," said Sister severely, "with what Miriam spends on that junk."

"It's not junk!"

"It is when she doesn't wear it! That's probably the first time those things have ever been worn since she bought them."

"I have to take them off," said Lilah with a sigh.

"Lilah!" Miriam called from the hall. "We got to get going!"

Lilah started to turn away, but Sister's hand shot out from beneath the light coverlet and grabbed her arm.

"Your daddy's lonely," Sister said in a low voice.

"Ma'am?"

"Your daddy's lonely since your mama got drowned in the Perdido."

"Yes, ma'am..." agreed Lilah tentatively, also in a low voice.

"That was two years ago, wasn't it? Two years ago last May."

"Yes, ma'am."

"I'm surprised he's not married yet."

"Married? Who would Daddy get married to?" asked Lilah in all surprise.

Sister looked closely at Lilah, and then looked significantly at the door.

Lilah followed that gaze uncomprehendingly.

"Who?" she asked again.

Sister nodded, but wouldn't speak.

"You mean Daddy might marry *Miriam?*"

"Who else?"

"Daddy's not gone marry *Miriam,*" exclaimed Lilah. "Who told you *that?*"

"Nobody told me. Nobody had to tell me. Y'all think just because I'm confined to my bed of pain that I don't know anything, that I don't see anything. Well, I do. Queenie tells me everything I need to hear. I have visitors. I have my own eyes, looking out this window. And I have the leisure to figure things out. I am gone be real surprised if you don't have a new mama before long."

"Sister," said Lilah, "I *cain't* believe it. I'm gone ask Miriam."

"If you do, she'll deny it. She won't give me the satisfaction of saying I was right. But one of these days you're gone walk in from the school, and your Daddy is gone say, 'Lilah, honey, Miriam and I have just run off and gotten ourselves married.' You see if he doesn't."

"I still don't think so."

"Don't you want those earrings?" Sister flicked a bony finger against the bob on Lilah's left ear. Lilah winced.

"Yes, ma'am. Course I do."

"If Miriam becomes your mama, you'll get those when she dies. You'll be heiress to a fortune in gems."

Lilah looked very doubtful about Sister's predictions. Miriam called out again.

17

"I got to go," said Lilah, pulling away.

Sister smiled knowingly and let go of Lilah's arm. Lilah ran out of the room. Miriam waited in the hallway and snatched the bobs from Lilah's ears and dropped them into her pocket. "Elinor's gone kill us," she said to Lilah, "so let's get a move on."

In Perdido's opinion, Billy Bronze had insufficiently mourned the death of his wife. Frances Caskey drowned in the Perdido one stormy night in the spring of 1956. Billy had been away at the time. Desultorily, the Perdido was dragged, above and below the junction, but Frances's body was not recovered. Elinor had told Billy of her daughter Frances's death: "She went out, Billy, the way she always did. But this time she just didn't come back."

Billy said, "It certainly wasn't like Frances to go off and drown herself. I never knew anybody who could swim better than she could. It stormed that night, you said. Maybe she got hit by lightning."

Billy's grief was quiet. He went to work as usual, his routines were unaltered, his appetite was unaffected, he never seemed distracted at odd moments. He slept alone at night now, and that seemed the main difference in his life. Perdido saw this apparent unfeelingness in Billy, and thought ill of him for it. Yet the Caskeys stood up for Billy. With a quiet word or two here and there, Elinor and Queenie reminded the town just how distant Frances had been in the last few years of her life, how she had begun to ignore both husband and daughter, how she had seemed to care for nothing but the river.

Billy, though he may have been alienated from his wife, certainly remained on good terms with the rest of the family. That relationship was unchanged by his wife's death. He remained in the house with his mother- and father-in-law, Elinor and Oscar, and gave no thought to moving anywhere else. When Oscar pointed out that some trouble might arise from

18

the problem of Frances's body never having been found, Billy only asked, "What sort of trouble?"

"Well," said Oscar uncomfortably, "in case you wanted to get married again..."

"Married!" laughed Billy. "Who on earth am I supposed to get married to, Oscar?"

"I don't know," said Oscar, "but there might be somebody, someday. I don't see it, I admit, but it might come about. Someday."

Billy laughed again. "Elinor wouldn't let me." And he shrugged an intelligible shrug, signifying, *and I wouldn't want her to, either.*

Billy's relationship with Miriam in these first two years of his widowerhood was the same as it always had been. They were as friendly, as intimate, and as businesslike as ever. It had never occurred to anyone, until it occurred to Sister, that there might be the possibility of a marriage between Billy Bronze and his sister-in-law. Lilah had no strong feelings about what the consequences of such a union might be, but had vague thoughts that they *might* be bad. So she went to her grandmother, and said, "Is Daddy gone marry Miriam? And if he marries her, does that mean I automatically get her jewels when she dies?"

"Where on earth did you get such an idea?" Elinor asked her granddaughter.

"From Sister. Sister says it's just a matter of time before Daddy and Miriam run off together. Are they gone live over here, or are they gone live next door?"

Elinor said, "I don't want to hear another word about this. It's not polite."

"Not polite?" asked Lilah, bewildered.

"Not polite," Elinor repeated, and for a time that was an end to the question for Lilah.

But not for Elinor. Elinor went to Oscar, and asked, "Have you heard anything about Billy marrying Miriam?"

Oscar hadn't heard of it. Neither had Queenie, or Lucille, or Grace, or Zaddie, or Ivey. Elinor called

19

on Sister, and said, "Where did you get such an idea, Sister?"

Sister leaned importantly back on her pillows, and said with an air of mystery, "I know what I know..."

"Oscar," said Elinor, unsatisfied, "talk to Miriam. You're the only one in this family she'll listen to."

"What difference does it make whether Billy marries Miriam or not?" Oscar asked.

"I'm not sure," Elinor conceded, "but we ought to see if we can find out one way or the other."

That evening, then, at the dinner table, while Zaddie was clearing before dessert, Oscar cleared his throat, and said, "Miriam, can I ask you a question without your jumping down my throat?"

"I don't know," said Miriam, not one to be trapped as easily as that. "Maybe. Maybe not. What's the question?"

"Well..." said Oscar hesitantly, "maybe I should ask Billy instead."

Billy glanced at Oscar, then at Miriam, and said, "Ask me, sure. I won't get mad."

"I'll ask both of you, then," said Oscar, then hesitated. Zaddie stood in the doorway, stacks of dishes piled high in both hands.

"Get on, Mr. Oscar," Zaddie said, "'fore I break every one of these plates."

"We've been wondering..."

"Who's been wondering?" asked Miriam.

"All of us," blurted Malcolm, and blushed.

"Wondering what?" said Billy.

"Wondering if the two of you were planning on running off and getting married."

Billy and Miriam looked at each other in amazement.

"Y'all have been sitting around the house thinking about *that?*" said Miriam after a few moments of stunned silence.

"Miriam and me?" croaked Billy.

"Sister said it," cried Queenie.

"Sister," said Miriam sharply, "has forgotten that

20

there is another world down at the other end of that hallway."

"Then you're not?" asked Lilah.

"Of course not," said Miriam. "That's the biggest piece of foolishness I have ever heard. Why on *earth* would I want to marry Billy?"

"Well, you're together all the time," said Queenie. "And Billy's lonely and sad without Frances. You're always making trips together anyway, so you might as well be married. Billy wouldn't marry anybody except a Caskey, and you wouldn't take the trouble to go after some man that was a stranger to you."

"Those are Sister's ideas," said Elinor.

"Well, they are completely wrong," said Miriam. "I cain't speak for Billy—"

"Yes, you can," said Billy quickly.

"—but we have never even thought of getting married, and we're not about to get married now."

"I miss Frances," said Billy, "but I've got Lilah here to keep me company. I don't need another wife. And I wouldn't *think* of bringing some woman here y'all didn't know anything about."

"Wouldn't have her anyway," snapped Elinor.

"I know that," said Billy, "and I'm not about to give y'all up just to have somebody to keep my feet warm at night."

So yet another of Sister's analyses was shattered, and the family was relieved. They weren't even quite sure *why* they were relieved, but they were. Zaddie took the dishes out, brought coffee, more plates, more forks, and then came in with a blackberry pie that was hot out of the oven; there was peach ice cream on the side.

Elinor poured coffee and passed it around. They talked of other things now, but Miriam was still and silent. She turned her cup around and around in its saucer and looked moodily about the room. Finally, when the conversation flagged for a moment, she glanced up and remarked, "Besides, you know, Billy and I *couldn't* get married."

21

"Why not?" said Queenie, whose most fervent purpose in life was to keep conversations going. "Because Frances hasn't been declared legally dead yet?"

"No," said Miriam. "Because I'm already engaged."

CHAPTER 73

Put It Off

Miriam looked around the table. "Well," she said after a moment, "isn't anybody going to bother to ask me who it is? I don't go off and get married *every* day, you know."

Everyone at the table was dumbfounded. If it wasn't Billy, then who on earth was Miriam going to wed?

"Who?" said Queenie at last. "Miriam, we are so happy for you, whoever it is, but..."

"But what?" said Miriam.

"But we had no idea," said Oscar.

Miriam shrugged. "Neither did I. I just decided. This minute. Y'all want me to get married so bad, guess I'll have to get married."

"Have you told the man?" asked Elinor.

"Not yet," said Miriam. "Maybe I ought to do that right now." She looked directly across the table at Malcolm, who had been silent and wide-eyed through all this, and said, "Malcolm, I accept your proposal." Then she turned her gaze first to Queenie on one side of Malcolm, and then to Elinor at the head of the table. "Which one of y'all wants to arrange the wedding?"

Queenie grabbed her son's arm beneath the tablecloth. "Malcolm!" she hissed. "What in the world do you mean by asking Miriam to marry you?"

"He is marrying me for my money, Queenie," said Miriam, unperturbed. "And because I tell him what to do. And 'cause he loves me, I guess. Malcolm needs somebody to keep him in line, and you're not always gone be around. You're an old woman, Queenie."

"I know that," returned Queenie. "But why are you accepting?"

"Because I probably *should* get married," said Miriam. "And because Malcolm is right here asking, and because y'all know that I am not about to put up with somebody who's gone cause me *one ounce* of trouble. And Malcolm," Miriam went on, eyeing her new fiancé across the table, "you are gone continue to do just what I tell you to, aren't you?"

"Yes, ma'am," said Malcolm with a somewhat overenthusiastic grin. "Mama, you are pinching me!"

Queenie let go of her son's arm.

"Queenie and I will take care of the wedding together," Elinor announced gravely. "Miriam, I think you've made a wise choice. We don't need any outsiders in this family." As she said this, she placed her hand gently over Billy Bronze's at her side, as if to reassure him that she did not think of *him* in that light.

Lilah, who sat next to her father on the other side, looked up at him and whispered, "Daddy, are you disappointed?" She didn't mean for anyone else at the table to hear her question, but they all did.

Billy laughed and put his arm around Lilah. "Lord, no!" he exclaimed. "I've got Miriam on my back enough as it is! You think I want to *live* with her? Malcolm, you're going to have a rough row to hoe!"

Malcolm only grinned. "I'm gone be forty next month. Miriam's gone be thirty-seven in the spring. 'Bout time we settled down."

"Almost too late to have children," sighed Queenie. "I was hoping for another little grandchild. But, Miriam, if you got started quick—"

"Queenie, you shut up about children," said Miriam. "I see one of those things in my house, I'm gone be using its head for a pincushion. Malcolm, don't you let Queenie put any ideas in your head about giving her grandchildren, because nobody is going to force *me* into a maternity wardrobe."

"Malcolm," asked Oscar, "where do you and Miriam intend on living?"

"Oscar, don't start asking me questions about all this. I just now found out about it myself. You want information, you ask Miriam. Miriam," he said diffidently, "you thought about where you want us to live?"

"I don't know," said Miriam. "Sister doesn't have a very high opinion of you, and I don't know how she'd take you moving in over there. And your mama wouldn't particularly care to have *me* underfoot." Here Queenie began a protest, but Miriam cut her off. "Don't bother to say anything sweet, Queenie, 'cause nobody at this table would believe it."

"I wasn't gone ask you to come live with me, Miriam. I was just gone ask you if you had spoken to Sister about any of this?"

"I have not," said Miriam. She pushed back her chair. "So I guess I better do that right now. Tell Zaddie to keep some coffee warm. I don't know how soon I'll be back."

Sister didn't like it one little bit. Miriam sat in a straight-backed chair by the door and fiddled with the dial on the radio, though she didn't turn on the set. Sister railed.

"I thought you were gone marry Billy!" cried Sister. "Billy's a man! Malcolm Strickland is no good, and has been no good since the day Queenie Strickland set foot in Perdido. I first saw Malcolm at Genevieve's funeral, and I said to Mama, 'Mama, that child is gone come to no good.' It was James and Dollie Faye Crawford kept that boy out of prison. It was you and Billy got him out from behind the counter of a barbecue joint in Mississippi. It has taken all the Caskeys together to keep that boy out of trouble for the past ten years."

25

"Malcolm's not a boy anymore, Sister. Malcolm's gone be forty years old next month."

"And what does he have to show for it?"

"He doesn't need anything to show for it. We're all rich, and perfectly capable of taking care of him. He's a lot of help around here, you know. He does lots of things that need doing. He keeps the roof in repair. He goes out and buys light bulbs. Why, he was in here last week, killing a bat that came down your chimney. You were glad enough to see him then."

"Oh, he's fine when it comes to killing bats," said Sister sarcastically. "But I don't know that that's much of a recommendation when it comes to marriage."

"I've met plenty of men who weren't even *that* much use," Miriam said. "At any rate, it doesn't really matter to me what you've got to say about it, Sister, 'cause I've made up my mind to marry Malcolm. And that's what I'm gone do."

"When did he ask you?" said Sister after a moment. Curiosity had got the upper hand over displeasure.

"Last week. Last month. Last year. Malcolm's been asking me to marry him for ten years. Malcolm brings me my mail in the morning, and says, 'Good morning, Miriam. Will you marry me?'"

"They why did you all of a sudden say yes?"

"Because I looked at my birth certificate the other day and I saw how old I was and I thought, *It's about time, Miriam*. And one day, I walked in here, and I saw how old you were, Sister."

"How old I am!"

Miriam nodded. "And I thought, *Someday Sister's gone die, and then I'm gone be left all alone*."

This casual observation about her mortality shocked Sister into a horrified silence. When she finally spoke her voice was weak and she was not at all to the point. "Miriam, will you *please* keep your hands off that radio. You are driving me crazy."

26

Miriam dropped her hand from the dial and then continued, glancing out the window as she spoke. "I've never lived by myself. I got to thinking what it would be like to be in this house all by myself. And I don't think I'd like it. I'd probably go crazy. And I'm much too busy to waste my time going crazy."

"So why didn't you just wait till I was dead before you got married?" said Sister. "Then you wouldn't have to deal with Malcolm until you had gotten me out of the way."

Miriam laughed. "Oh, Sister, you don't bother me anymore. And neither does Malcolm."

"I don't think I want Malcolm Strickland in this house," said Sister. "His tread is too heavy."

"Then we'll move in next door with Queenie and leave you here alone."

"No!" shouted Sister, suddenly panicked. "Miriam, why don't you put off the marriage for a little while?"

"Till you're dead?"

"No," answered Sister, calming a bit, "just till I'm used to the idea. Just for a little while, Miriam. I'm confined to this bed. It's so hard for me to change. I cain't even *think* of you getting married. You're still my little girl."

Miriam turned from the window and smiled.

"What are you laughing about?" demanded Sister.

"At you. You're trying to get me to put off my wedding, just like Grandmama tried to get you to put off your wedding to Early."

"Mama was right! See what a mess I made of it? If I had listened to Mama, I'd be a happy woman today! So you ought to listen to me, and put this wedding off. Just for a while. Just till you've thought about it some more."

"No," said Miriam easily, walking toward the door. "I've made up my mind, and that is that."

And that *was* that. The ability the Caskeys had to astonish Perdido seemed inexhaustible. The announcement of the engagement of Malcolm Strickland and Miriam Caskey was a source of vast wonder in the town. Previously there had been two local theories when it came to the question of Miriam's marriage. Half the town thought she would marry Billy Bronze, and the other half was certain she would never marry at all. That she would marry Malcolm Strickland was a possibility that had occurred to no one. The only satisfactory explanation Perdido could come up with was that Malcolm had raped Miriam, and that she was pregnant.

Miriam wasn't a woman for long engagements. She announced that the wedding would take place two days after Christmas, a date she chose for the practical reason that her calendar was clear for the holiday and the few days on either side of it. "I have no intention," Miriam told her mother, "of calling up people in Houston and New York to rearrange my appointments just because I'm getting married."

That gave Elinor and Queenie just two months to make all the arrangements, but they went at it with a will. The wedding itself—like all the Caskey ceremonies—was to be a small and private affair, held at ten in the morning in the living room at Elinor's. The reception, however, was a different matter. It was Queenie's idea, originally, that for a change they should throw a proper party—"With everybody in Perdido and beyond invited," as she put it. Queenie had really never expected Miriam to go along with this idea for a minute; she had been certain that Miriam would want everything as brief and casual as possible. But Miriam surprised her future mother-in-law. "Good idea. Invite everybody," she said. And everyone *was* invited. More than five hundred invitations to the reception went out. Miriam was a businesswoman, and as such she was well known all over southern Alabama, the Florida panhandle, and much farther afield. She recognized that she had a position to maintain, and that position dictated that her wedding be in keeping with her stature. The bridegroom, it was true, was not all that he might have been, but all Miriam's business associates had seen Malcolm in tow at one time or another. Most, if the truth be told, conjectured that Miriam kept him around for more reasons than the fact that he knew how to change a light bulb.

Oscar was away much of the time between the announcement of Miriam's engagement and the wedding itself. Elinor saw to that; she wanted him out of the way so that she could do what needed to be done. She suggested that he see what the golf courses were like in Kentucky, and Luvadia allowed her son Sammy to accompany Mr. Oscar as his caddy. Oscar's eyes were poor, and he needed someone who was familiar and patient with his infirmity. For those two months, Oscar and Sammy—who was only four-teen, and illegally out of school for this time—drove around Georgia and South Carolina, and Oscar played at country clubs and public links all over both states. Oscar put up in motels and hotels, sneaking Sammy to his room at night, the boy sleeping on the floor, rolled in blankets. Oscar called Perdido every day and asked Elinor if things had quieted down enough for him to come home. Her invariable reply was, "Stay away as long as you can, darling. You'll just be trampled underfoot down here."

Miriam wouldn't help with anything, but insisted on maintaining her schedule at the mill. She and Malcolm and Billy made two trips to Houston, and one to Atlanta in those short eight weeks. Her wedding dress was fitted in her office while she was recording letters into a Dictaphone.

Malcolm was helplessly happy. He could scarcely believe his good fortune. He worried a bit about whether or not he would make a good husband, but then reflected that this was none of his concern, really. Miriam would make of him what she wanted. With this bolstering reasoning, he gave himself up completely to his contentment. His relationship with Miriam was unchanged, with a single exception:

29

when he and Miriam and Billy traveled together, it was now Malcolm and Miriam who put up in the double room and Billy who took single. Before, Billy had always shared the room with Miriam. Queenie had once asked Miriam why she didn't let Malcolm and Billy share the double on these trips, and take the single herself. That surely had a better *appearance*. Queenie had received an unexpected reply: "Queenie, the truth is that I'm afraid to sleep alone. And I'm old enough and rich enough to do what I want."

Malcolm, now that he shared a room with Miriam, made no attempt to sleep in her bed. He would be guided by her in *that* business as well.

Queenie remained bewildered by all these new circumstances. But she stayed busy—there was so little time, and *so* much to be done—and gave herself little time for reflection. Nevertheless, when she sat still for a few moments, she could scarcely credit her son's engagement. He wasn't marrying Miriam for her money, of that Queenie was certain. Queenie herself was rich now, and she had assured Malcolm that her will provided amply for him. She could not bring herself to believe, however, that Malcolm really loved his bride-to-be. Yet perhaps he did, and perhaps she even loved him. Queenie would sigh. All this was beyond her, and it was much easier to worry about getting the napkins printed in time.

On the Saturday after Thanksgiving, Lucille and Grace hosted a shower for Miriam, and every woman of any social standing in Perdido was pleased to attend. Lucille and Grace had always been reclusive outside the family, and many in Perdido had never visited Gavin Pond Farm before. The place was changed out of all recognition from what it once had been. The little farm house that pregnant Lucille had entered with such misgiving fourteen years before had been spruced up and added onto in so many different directions that it looked like a different place altogether. A blacktop lane lead to it from the main road, there was a huge brick patio and a large swimming pool. Two acres of woods had been cleared for a camellia garden, and Lucille was busily establishing some of the rarest species known. An enormous herd of cows grazed in the pecan orchard, and the place boasted three cars, two trucks, two tractors, and five different boats. At night, the sky south of Gavin Pond Farm was orange with the light of the burn-off flares of the oil wells in the swamp.

Grace was forty-six, thinner than any Caskey had ever been—gaunt, actually. She was burned by the sun, and made happy by Lucille. Lucille was thirty-eight, fatter than Queenie, and made happy by Grace. Lucille's boy, Tommy Lee Burgess, was now fourteen. Shy, good-natured, and bumbling, he was an odd member of the family; not paid much attention to when he was about, and altogether forgotten when he was not. Tommy Lee loved to fish, hunt, drive cars, and be by himself. Grace once asked him if he maybe wanted to be sent to military school, where he'd be around some men for a change, but Tommy Lee shook his head in horror, and said he didn't want to go anywhere or do anything else than what he was doing.

Grace and Lucille had built Luvadia the biggest kitchen anybody in those parts had ever seen, and Zaddie and Melva came out to help with the food for the shower. The ladies of Perdido showed up half an hour early in hopes that they would be shown around the place. Lucille was proud of her house, and happy to comply. The ladies were impressed, and playfully chastised Grace and Lucille for keeping this wonderful place such a secret.

In the midst of the festivities Grace said to Miriam, "This place started out a secret, what with Lucille coming out here when she was pregnant. And then when we found oil, we wanted to keep *that* secret for a while. So Lucille and I just got in the habit of living here all by ourselves, and never hav-

31

ing anybody but family. Maybe we ought to start entertaining a little more."

"Wouldn't catch me doing for this pack," said Miriam in a low voice, gazing around at the crowd of women bent over the food on the dining room table.

The charade played out by Miriam when she sat down and opened her gifts far outdid any of the performances the ladies put on during a real game of charades later. Miriam looked with excitement on a new adding machine, but she didn't see much good in pink underwear and fuzzy bathroom slippers. She was, however, as gracious as she was capable of being, and afterward even Elinor went so far as to say, "You could have made things very unpleasant, but you didn't."

"There was no point," said Miriam. "They were being nice to me."

"Sometimes," said Elinor, "I think you may be growing up."

"The question is," sighed Miriam, "how the hell am I gone get rid of all that damned *junk?*"

Sister could not be reconciled to the wedding. She would have nothing to do with it, and she wouldn't hear it spoken of in her presence. She refused even to admit aloud that Miriam was marrying Malcolm. Queenie had been forced to desert her in this busy time, so the whole thing rankled even more. Ivey sat with Sister every day, in the straight chair beside the radio, but Ivey wasn't one for gossip, and Sister was bored and restless and stared out the window through binoculars at Elinor's house. But she never saw more than Zaddie or Elinor occasionally passing a window.

Ivey wouldn't relay any news from next door, for her feud with Zaddie had kept up, and they were not speaking. No one had ever discovered the reason for this coolness between the aging black sisters, for it was a private affair, and neither Zaddie nor Ivey ever said anything about it directly.

In the drawer of her bedside table, Sister kept a calendar on which she marked off the days until Christmas, and every day she would count up those remaining. This ever-decreasing figure preyed on her mind to an extent that Ivey found alarming. Ivey began to ply Sister with sweet liquids poured out of unmarked blue bottles, but these nostrums did not appear to help. Sister grew weaker—but crosser—and every morning she seemed to have sunk down deeper into her bulwark of goose-down pillows.

About ten days before the wedding, Miriam went to New Orleans on an unexpected and unavoidable trip. When she returned at suppertime two days later, Ivey was waiting for her behind the screen door. "Miz Caskey sick," she said simply. "She want to talk to you."

Upstairs, Miriam was shocked by Sister's appearance. "You *are* sick," she said bluntly. "I don't think I've ever seen anybody look worse."

Sister seemed scarcely able to open her eyes. Her head lolled forward on her neck; her hands lay curled and helpless atop the neatly folded coverlet. She looked as if she had not moved for days, a frail puppet whose strings had all been cut.

"Put it off," she whispered. Her lips scarcely moved. Miriam moved closer to the bed.

"Put it off," Sister repeated, no more loudly than before.

"No," said Miriam, finally comprehending the cryptic command. "For one thing, Elinor and Queenie have gone to a great deal of trouble. For another thing, it's too late. And last of all, I want to go through with it."

Sister's head lolled to one side. "It'll kill me," she whispered. Her head lolled to the other side, and her eyes shut with the motion.

Miriam sat on the edge of the bed. It was dark outside, and a single low lamp burned on the bedside table. Miriam took Sister's hand. "Sister," she said firmly, "even if I believed that, I'd go through with it."

Sister opened her eyes slowly, and peered up at Miriam through tears. "You'd kill me, wouldn't you?"

"Sister," said Miriam, now taking her other hand, and pressing them lightly against Sister's breast, "you are turning into Grandmama."

"Noooo..." Sister's protest was no more than a slow exhalation of breath.

"You are. You want to trick me into putting this wedding off. Just the way Grandmama would have done. But you're not Grandmama, you're Sister. And I'm not you, I'm not Oscar. I'm not even me when I was younger. Nobody's going to run roughshod over me—not about this, and not about anything else. You think you can get me to put off this wedding by pulling this business—"

"Not business..."

"Whether it is or it isn't is of no concern to me," Miriam went on. "If you're really sick, then I'm sorry, but it makes no difference. I won't let it. So you might as well get better, Sister, because next Saturday night there are going to be four hundred and thirty-seven people tromping through this house giving me their congratulations, and I wouldn't want the noise to disturb you."

Miriam released Sister's hands, then rose and walked out the door and down the hall to her own room to unpack.

"Put it off," whispered Sister Haskew a few moments later, not realizing that Miriam was no longer in the room.

CHAPTER 74

The Wedding Party

Sister's condition remained the same in the week before the wedding. Oscar, on his return, was shocked to find her so deplorably weak and wandering. Christmas came and after presents had been opened at Elinor's in the morning, everyone went over to give Sister her gifts, congregating in the hallway outside her room, but entering only one at a time. Sister smiled wanly, but she wasn't always able to open her eyes. Lilah sat on the edge of the bed and placed a wrapped box on Sister's upturned hand. One finger clawed briefly at the ribbon, but then Lilah had to open it herself. It was a box of Sister's favorite powder, that smelled of dead roses. "Thank you, child," Sister whispered, and her eyes, wet with tears, flickered open briefly.

No one, not even Elinor, dared suggest that the wedding be postponed on account of Sister's illness. Miriam had been preternaturally good about all the wedding arrangements, acquiescing to each and every suggestion put forth by Elinor or Queenie, but who knew what might happen if Miriam were asked to put off the date of her marriage to Malcolm Strickland? She might not go through with it at all. She might cart Malcolm off to a justice of the peace, and never come home afterward. She would certainly never set foot in Sister's room again. "And I'm not sure Miriam's not right," sighed Oscar, who was much affected by his sister's increased infirmity. "I remember how I put off and put off to please Mama, and it got us into nothing but trouble."

Elinor did not contradict him, and the wedding remained scheduled for Saturday.

The day after Christmas, workers from the mill came and erected open-sided tents in the yards behind all three of the Caskey houses, using the tall, narrow trunks of the water oaks as poles. The striped canvas tents stretched from the back porches of the houses all the way to the levee. A stage was erected on the edge of the forest, and here the small orchestra from Mobile would play. Malcolm was in charge of chairs and tables, and he had gathered them from churches, armories, and VFW halls all over the county. These preparations were of great interest to Perdido, and cars drove slowly up and down the road in front of the house all day long. Children sat perched on the fence around the orchard across the way, wearing their new Christmas clothes and showing off to one another their new toys as they watched the proceedings.

During all of this, Oscar felt only that he was in the way—in his own home—and the only place he might be *out* of the way was with Sister. So he made his way over to her house and sat at her side, talking of old times. Only occasionally would Sister respond to her brother's long stories and reminiscences, and rarely in a voice loud enough for him to make out the words. And when he did understand her, he shifted uncomfortably in his chair, for it appeared to him that Sister hadn't comprehended a word he had said to her. Yet there he continued to sit. He held Sister's hand, and he talked about the years in which he and Sister had grown up in this house with their mother Mary-Love. "And, Sister, you know what?" he said. "You're getting to look more and more like her every day."

All the Caskey cooks working for weeks together wouldn't have been able to prepare food for the crowd of people that was anticipated, and the caterers began arriving soon after dawn on Saturday morning.

The day was overcast and dim, though warm. The

36

caterers worried about rain, but the Caskeys had no fear. Elinor had declared, succinctly but with absolute authority, "No rain today."

At nine o'clock, Elinor and Queenie, already in their finery, converged on Miriam's house and went upstairs to help Miriam into her dress. They found her struggling into it without ceremony or sentiment. "Damn! Damn! Damn!" she cried. "Don't people know enough to take the damned pins out?"

She was ready in another quarter-hour, and there was nothing to do but sit and wait until ten o'clock. Miriam sat impatiently by the window, beating her bouquet in the palm of her hand and occasionally calling out greetings to one of the workmen passing by below. Queenie went home to make certain that Malcolm got his tie on straight. Lucille and Grace came by, kissed Miriam, and said, "You are making a great mistake getting married to a man. We hope you're gone be the happiest woman in the world."

A few minutes before it was time to go next door, Elinor got up and shut the door, then strode back across the room and stood before her daughter. She and Miriam were alone.

"Well?" said Miriam impatiently. "Am I unzipped?"

"You look beautiful," said Elinor quietly. "I just wanted to ask you what you and Malcolm are doing about a ring?"

Miriam laughed, and pointed at the dresser in the corner of the room. "Go ask Lilah if I don't have a whole damned case full of rings in the bottom drawer over there—and that's not to mention my safety-deposit boxes. I reached in there and pulled one out and gave it to Malcolm. No reason in putting out good money when I've got so many already."

"Miriam," said Elinor, "you know I haven't given you anything yet."

"Well, you've arranged all this," said Miriam, waving her hand inclusively toward the window. Below were the striped tents, a dozen servants and

37

hired men; the sound of rattling bottles and a murmur of directives floated up. "I couldn't have done all that."

"I have something else for you though."

"What?" asked Miriam suspiciously.

"This," said Elinor, reaching into her purse and drawing out a simple diamond ring. The solitaire was cloudy but large, nearly three karats; the setting a four-pronged gold band. Miriam took it from her mother slowly, fingered the facets of the jewel, and then glaced back up at Elinor.

"This was Grandmama's," said Miriam slowly. "You took it off her when she was lying in the coffin. Before I got there."

"That's right," said Elinor.

"I have never forgiven you for that."

"I know," said Elinor.

"It didn't matter that you were the one who told me where the oil was down below Gavin Pond Farm, it didn't matter that you never tried to interfere with me in the running of the mill, it didn't matter that you kept this family together and made everybody pretty much happy—I have never forgiven you for taking this ring."

Elinor said nothing.

"I suppose," said Miriam, "that you want me to forgive you now."

"I don't expect that," said Elinor. "But it was right that you should have the ring, now that you're getting married."

Miriam glanced out of the window. "It's getting time," she said. "I'm going to have to go speak to Sister." She slipped the ring on her finger, rose and went out of the room, leaving her mother alone.

Miriam stood at the side of Sister's bed, holding her bouquet in her hands before her. It was the fragrance of those fresh flowers, so pervasive in the room that for so many years had smelled of only dead blossoms, that caused Sister's eyes to open.

"Sister," said Miriam, "I'm going over to Elinor's now, and Malcolm and I are gone get married."

Sister tried to turn away her head, but hadn't the strength. Her eyes fell shut again.

"We'll spend the afternoon getting ready for the reception this evening, and then after that Malcolm and I are taking off for New Orleans for our honeymoon. We were gone go to New York, but there's some business I need to get done in New Orleans, so we changed our plans. Malcolm says we'll go anywhere I want to go, and if I don't want to go anywhere we can stay right here. Queenie's gone stay with you while I'm gone, the way she always does. And when we get back, I'm moving Malcolm in over here. I haven't decided yet whether he's gone stay in my room, or whether I'm gone put him across the hall. But that doesn't matter to you, I guess, since you never get out of this room anyway. You don't have to worry about Malcolm, because I've already told him to leave you alone, and not come near you unless you call him. And he's already bought three new pairs of shoes with soft soles, so he won't be stomping through the house the way he usually does."

By no movement or other sign did Sister indicate she had heard a thing Miriam had said to her.

"Elinor just gave me Mama's ring, Sister. I thought that ring was gone forever. It's bigger than I remembered it, but the stone is flawed."

Sister still did not move. Her hands lay lifeless atop the coverlet.

Miriam suddenly turned and dragged a chair up to the bed. She tossed her bouquet aside. She sat in the chair, reached forward, and grasped both Sister's hands and squeezed them.

"Your blessing!" she hissed. "Give me your blessing, Sister!"

Sister slowly opened her eyes, and even more slowly, she shook her head no.

* * *

The wedding ceremony was quiet and hurried. Ruthie Driver officiated. Ruthie, as everyone had predicted, had grown up to be just like her mother, Annie Bell. When Annie Bell Driver died, Ruthie took over the pastorship for the Zion Grace Baptist Church. Now she was married herself, but most people were hard put to remember her husband's name. Neither Miriam nor Malcolm attended Ruthie's church, but Miriam said she felt more comfortable being married by a woman. Billy Bronze was Malcolm's best man, and Lilah was the single bridesmaid. Oscar and Elinor held hands, as did Grace and Lucille. Tommy Lee put his arm around Queenie's heaving shoulders. The only music was that of a carpenter's last-minute hammering outside.

"All right," said Miriam, as soon as Ruthie had cried *Amen* to her prayer, "let's get this show on the road."

Everyone ran home and changed out of their stiff clothes, and reappeared a few minutes later, ready to help with the final preparations for the reception that evening. Oscar took himself up to Sister's room, and listened to a football game on the radio. Elinor and Queenie seemed to be everywhere at once, and there was so much to do and see to, that for the first time in more than ten years Ivey and Zaddie found themselves speaking to each other. Grace and Lucille systematically set tasks for themselves, and calmly carried them out one by one; they set up the punch tables, found the right tablecloths, unwrapped and washed all of James's hundreds and hundreds of cut-glass punch cups. Even Lilah was busy, ordering about men who were three times her age, and feeling very important about it all. Miriam roamed about with Malcolm more or less in tow, saying a word here and there to the caterers, the servants, and the mill workers, not bothering to help with anything herself, but evidently enjoying herself greatly. "It just feels so good to be out of that damned dress," she said several times. She wore Mary-Love's

40

diamond ring on her finger, but she avoided speaking to her mother.

By four o'clock, everything was ready. Lilah ran upstairs at Sister's and said to Oscar, "Granddaddy, Grandmama says it's time to go home and get dressed. People are gone be coming up any time now."

Oscar rose, went to Sister's side, and said, "Sister, is all this gone bother you? Are you gone be disturbed having so many people about?"

Sister didn't respond, but Oscar felt the slightest pressure of her fingers against the palm of his hand. He hadn't any idea how to interpret that.

The first guests arrived half an hour early, which was only to be expected. It was impossible for those coming from long distances to time arrivals exactly. Queenie's entire house had been set up as a kind of retiring room for gentlemen, while Miriam's was given over to the ladies. Elinor and Oscar and Queenie, as parents of the wedded couple, received in the formal rooms of Elinor's house. Miriam was dressed in green silk, and wore no other jewelry than Mary-Love's solitaire, her simple wedding-band, and a single bracelet of emeralds. Malcolm, who had grown accustomed to wearing a suit, appeared serene in his new character as husband of the heiress. The guests agreed that Malcolm wasn't the brightest man in the world, that he wasn't the husband for *every* woman, and that he doubtless would be led a merry dance by his wife, but they also agreed that, on the whole, he was exactly suited to the position to which Miriam had raised him. No one was surprised when she sent him off to refill her punch cup, to get her three petit fours of the type she liked best, to ask Elinor if the man from Texas National Oil had arrived yet. This was exactly her treatment of him before their marriage, and everyone had assumed that this was the way things would continue.

Dinner was served outside. The striped canvas tents billowed and peaked in the breeze and underneath, the trunks of the water oaks were like slim,

41

grotequesly curved columns. Sand got into everyone's shoes, but the hundreds of yellow lights provided warm, flattering illumination, and for once the smell of the Perdido, flowing closely at hand behind the levee, was sweet, as if specially perfumed for the occasion.

Perdido was beside itself with pleasure at this grand party. Miriam had not made many demands concerning the preparations, but she had decreed that every mill worker receive an invitation. And so every mill worker—and every mill worker's wife—was there; most had bought new clothes for the occasion. There wasn't a one of them that Miriam didn't know by name. Oscar, in the receiving line, was shocked by the number he either had forgotten or had never known at all. Guests came from all over south Alabama and western Florida, arriving in caravans of cars from Mobile, Montgomery, and Pensacola. Oil and lumber men flew in from New York, Atlanta, New Orleans, and Houston. There was even an auxiliary tent set up behind Queenie's house for the black population of Perdido.

After the dinner was served, the mill workers took off their jackets, and quickly cleared away all the tables and chairs. The orchestra meanwhile tuned its instruments and began to play. Sammy Sapp and an army of black girls and boys raked the sand once again in preparation for the dancing. That was at nine o'clock, and Miriam declared that the music would play until the last couple dropped on their feet.

Miriam and Malcolm had the first dance, and were applauded and cheered for their expertise. Elinor and Queenie exchanged proud but slightly puzzled glances—neither of them had imagined that *those* two would have performed so creditably.

Oscar cut in, and danced off with Miriam. Malcolm bowed to Elinor, and brought her out onto the sand. Shortly thereafter, the dancing was general, and more than a thousand people waltzed in the sand among the water oaks.

Those who had lived in Perdido a long time marveled not at the splendor of the proceedings, for the Caskeys were very rich indeed, and could well afford this and much more besides, but rather that there was any party at all. No one could remember when any Caskey had been married off with any celebration whatsoever. Caskey weddings had always been simple if somewhat hugger-mugger affairs, and that Miriam of all people should have wanted—or even allowed—such an outlay as this was as astonishing a thing as Perdido was likely to see in a long while.

Because Miriam's house had been set aside for the ladies, there was throughout the evening a constant traipsing in and out the front door, in and out the back door, up and down the stairs, into and out of Miriam's room, the two guest rooms, and the two bathrooms. Before the party really got under way, Queenie had gone up and sat with Sister for a few minutes, thinking that she was paler and less responsive than ever. Queenie had also installed Luvadia's ten-year-old daughter, Versie, as a sort of guard for Sister, giving the child strict instructions to keep the door closed against all visitors. But Versie was a little country colored girl and no match for the ladies of Perdido, who knew Sister's room to be at the end of the hall. The ladies of Perdido were not slow in taking advantage of this unprecedented opportunity of peeking in and speaking to Sister Haskew, who hadn't been seen on the streets of Perdido in over ten years. They came singly at first, brushing aside Versie and sitting at the side of the bed for a few moments, speaking volubly to Sister, lamenting her ill health, and finally growing constrained when it became apparent that Sister was not going to respond in any way. Soon it seemed impossible to shut the door, and the ladies of Perdido swarmed into the room and surrounded Sister's bed. That room, visited so rarely in the past decade, became a welter of silks and wools, powders, and perfumes, gabble and laughter. Sister lay immobile, propped up against her wall of goose-down pillows, her hands upturned and curled on the neatly turned coverlet.

Versie grew so demoralized by her inability to keep out these women that at last she gave up the fight altogether, and sneaked away, down the stairs, out the back door, and into the tent reserved for the colored people. She hid in a shadowed corner, drank punch, and ate chicken until she couldn't eat or drink any more. She wasn't discovered until an hour later, by Oscar, whose dimming eyesight caused him to trip over her on his way to the bathroom in Queenie's house.

"Who is that?" he asked.

"It's Versie, Mr. Oscar," the child replied, frightened.

"Is that Luvadia's Versie?"

"Yes, sir."

"What are you doing here? Queenie told me she had put you upstairs with Sister."

"She did, Mr. Oscar," Versie replied, terrified at being discovered in the neglect of her duty, "but they was so many ladies in there, they 'bout drove me out!"

"What!" exclaimed Oscar. "You mean to say you let people get into that room?"

"I couldn't keep 'em out!"

"Versie, you go find Queenie and you get her up there and you get those women out of there, you hear me? *Right now!*"

Oscar went on to the bathroom, but when he was finished he went next door to Miriam's and went inside. The ladies screamed and laughed at a man in their midst, but Oscar paid no attention to them. He marched up the stairs and down the hall to Sister's room. Versie evidently hadn't found Queenie yet—or perhaps Versie was so afraid of Queenie's finding out what she had done that she had not sought

44

her at all—for the room was still crowded with women. They sat in the chairs, they leaned against the furniture, they perched on the windowsill and the edge of the bed. There in their midst lay Sister, silent and unmoving.

"Out!" cried Oscar loudly. "Everybody out!"

There was an excited protest, for Oscar's tone was rude and peremptory. Yet Oscar said nothing else. He simply took hold of the arm of the woman nearest him—the wife of one of the new doctors in town—and shoved her none too gently out the door.

"Well!" she cried, and turned around to object, but by then Oscar had grabbed a second woman, the mill accountant's wife, and shoved both women out into the hallway.

Now Oscar had his hands on a third; he kept repeating over and over again, "Out! Out! All of you out!" Seeing that he meant business, there was a general retreat to the door, and in only a few seconds more, the room was cleared. Oscar slammed the door shut, whipped the curtains closed, and he and his sister were alone. Oscar pulled a chair up close to the bed.

"Sister," he said in a low voice, "have you got your eyes open? It's so dark in here, I cain't hardly see."

Sister didn't move that Oscar could tell.

"I got 'em all out. Queenie had no business leaving Luvadia's Versie up here. That child is too small to bar a door. But don't you worry, 'cause I'm gone sit up here with you. And there's not one of them that's gone get past that door, not while I'm in here."

So, waiting for Queenie, Oscar sat back in the chair, and told Sister about the reception—how many people were there, and who had said what, and how pretty Miriam was, and how handsome Malcolm looked. He could hear the orchestra playing from its stage at the edge of the woods, and when he knew the words of the songs, he'd sing along for a while and smile at Sister and straighten her covers. After a while, though, he grew serious, and said, "I'm gone say something you don't want to hear, Sister, but it's

45

got to be said. And that's that you have treated Miriam badly about this whole business. Miriam didn't deserve to be treated badly, she has always been good to you. Miriam is sharp, but I don't believe that there was ever a human being on the face of this earth more faithful than Miriam. She would do anything for you, and you have treated her badly. You have been acting the way Mama would have acted. There's no other way to put it. You are getting to be just like Mama, and it has just about killed me to watch it happen. But here you are, and it's not too late to change, 'cause when Miriam and Malcolm come back from New Orleans, they're gone be right down there at the other end of the hall, and you're gone have twenty opportunities a day to be nice to them. And you could do it, if you put your mind to it. I cain't speak for Miriam, whether she really loves Malcolm or not, and I cain't speak for Malcolm, whether he loves Miriam or not. But it looks that way, despite what any of us ever thought about either of them. And they deserve every chance in the world of being happy. I have never said this, Sister, I have never even said this to Elinor, but it hurt me, and it hurt me bad, when you and Mama took Miriam away from Elinor and me. I watched her grow up over here knowing that she was mine, knowing that she had been taken away from me and that she would never ever belong to me again. That hurt me bad, and even Frances couldn't make up for it. Billy doesn't make up for it, Lilah doesn't make up for it. When you took Miriam away from me, that was a loss that I have never gotten over, not to this very day, Sister. So you have an obligation—an obligation to *me*—to see to it that my little girl, my little girl who was taken away from me so many, many years ago, is happy. Sister," he said softly, "Sister, are you gone do it?"

He reached forward and grasped Sister's hands atop the coverlet, but they were already cold and stiff.

CHAPTER 75

Queenie Alone

Versie at last found Queenie in the crush of the reception and told her that Mr. Oscar wanted her upstairs in Sister's room. Queenie didn't pause even to try to figure out why the black girl was trembling so, but hurried into Miriam's house and up the stairs, past women who complained to her of Oscar's rudeness to them. Queenie tried the door of the room but discovered it locked. She pounded on the door.

"Oscar!" she called. "Is that you in there with Sister?"

In a moment, she heard Oscar's low voice on the other side. "Go away, Queenie," he said. "Sister and I are talking."

"Are you all right?"

"We're fine," returned Oscar. He unlocked the door, and opened it a crack. Queenie thrust her head inside and peered beyond Oscar to the bed. There lay sister, still and silent.

"Well," whispered Queenie, "I am glad you are up here to keep her company. I know all this noise must be driving her right out of her head."

"Queenie, listen to me. I'm gone stay up here and talk to Sister, but you got to do a couple of things for me." There was an urgent tone in Oscar's voice that puzzled Queenie, but she only nodded acquiescence and asked no questions. "See if you can get hold of Ivey or Zaddie or Luvadia and get one of them up here. Then tell Elinor to come up. But most important, tell Malcolm that he and Miriam are *not* to take off for New Orleans till they've seen me. And they are not to go till the last damn guest has gone home."

Oscar started to shut the door, but Queenie jammed her foot into the crack and pushed the door back a bit. She peered around the door again at Sister on the bed, shifted her gaze back at Oscar, and then said, "All right, Oscar."

Zaddie and Ivey arrived at Sister's room and were ensconced on chairs on either side of Sister's door for the rest of that evening; none of the ladies of Perdido got near enough even to knock. Elinor arrived, went into the room, and came out again a few minutes later. After that, Grace and Lucille did the same. Billy Bronze entered the room and remained with Oscar. A rumor began circulating around the party that Sister Haskew was fuming and uncontrollable, and that the Caskeys were desperately attempting to dissuade her from calling in a lawyer and disinheriting Miriam. People glanced sidewise at Miriam and wondered that she herself didn't go upstairs and try to pacify her aunt with outpourings of undiminished affection.

The reception began to wind down; by half past one the last few guests had wandered off to try to find their automobiles. The orchestra and the caterers packed up and headed back to Mobile and Pensacola, and the striped canvas tents drooped in the late night air. The old pungent smell of the Perdido returned and washed over the Caskey landscape, and the detritus of the party—the grandest celebration that Perdido had ever seen—seemed sad and bleak.

Miriam and Malcolm were led upstairs by Queenie, through the wreckage wrought by the ladies of Perdido; past Lucille and Grace and Tommy Lee, sitting next to one another on the edge of Miriam's bed and staring morosely out into the hallway; past Billy Bronze with his arm around Lilah, standing in the door of the guest room. As they went by, Billy grabbed Malcolm's hand and pulled him aside. Queenie and

Miriam went on alone. They passed between Ivey and Zaddie—a black Gog and Magog—and into Sister's room. Oscar and Elinor sat on opposite sides of the bed, and Sister, propped against her palisade of pillows and with her hands curled and upturned on the neatly turned-down coverlet, lay cold and starkly dead.

Miriam and Billy didn't go on their honeymoon to New Orleans. It was announced the next day that Sister Haskew had died late in the night. Perdido was told that the anticipation of Miriam's wedding, and the splendid reception, had served to keep Sister alive for no one knew how many months. Sister had died a happy woman, with all her family at her side. She was buried on the twenty-ninth of December in the Caskey plot in the Perdido cemetery between James and Mary-Love.

Arriving home from the funeral, even before she had removed her veiled hat, Miriam marched down the hallway. Without even glancing inside, she pulled shut the door of Sister's room. Taking a key from her pocket she locked the door. Then she dropped the key to the floor, and kicked it through the crack under the door.

On the second of January, 1959, Miriam went to New Orleans. It was a business trip, but so that it would not appear that she and Malcolm were actually honeymooning so soon after Sister's death, Malcolm remained in Perdido. Billy went with her instead.

Ivey Sapp retired from service. She had stayed on, she said, only because Sister couldn't do without her. But her feet hurt her, and she forgot things. Besides, she was lonesome without Bray, and all she wanted to do was to sit at home and listen to the radio. Ivey had no money at all, but she was so confident that the Caskeys would provide for her, that she did not even bother to mention her needs when she spoke to Miriam. And she was right, for Miriam dropped by her humble home in Baptist Bottom the following week, ostensibly to fetch a recipe for fried corn for Melva, but actually to slip a substantial check under the corner of the tablecloth.

Miriam and Malcolm, tended by Melva, stayed on in the house, which was now considerably diminished in spirit by the departure of Sister and Ivey, who together had inhabited the place for more than a century. Miriam gave Malcolm the room directly across the hall from hers, also at the front of the house; but this was only where Malcolm kept his clothes and a few personal things. He slept with Miriam. After a week, Miriam declared that she didn't know why she hadn't got married before; sleeping with a man certainly was a great deal more fun than sleeping alone. "I don't know what it's gone be like in the summer, though. I guess we're gone have to get an air conditioner in here."

When Sister's will was probated late in the spring of 1959, it was found that with the exception of a substantial bequest to Ivey Sapp, all of Sister's property, holdings, stocks, and cash, went to Miriam. Miriam and Malcolm were now richer than ever. That appeared to make not one whit of difference to Miriam, and Malcolm had no conception of money beyond what Miriam had made plain to him: "Malcolm, you and I have got more than we would be able to spend in a thousand years."

It was Queenie who seemed most affected by Sister's death. This wasn't surprising, for Queenie's whole life had been wrapped up in Sister for the past ten years. When not actually nursing her, she had kept her company, operating as Sister's eyes and ears, bearing the brunt of Sister's displeasures, developing her patience and humility to an extraordinary degree.

All deaths are sudden, no matter how gradual the

dying may be. For over eleven years Sister had lain in that bed—on those five mattresses and those ten pillows—and the pattern of her days and years had been inexorable and unchanging. Gradually, the oscillations of that pendulum had grown weaker and weaker, but Queenie had hardly noticed the diminution of Sister's strength. And to have the pendulum stop was a great wrench indeed. Queenie had walked away from the funeral wondering what on earth she was to do with herself.

And Malcolm had now left her also. He had been with her for quite a while, and had served to fill out her meager household. Now he was at Miriam's, and had precious little to do with her anymore. Every time Queenie stepped out of her house, her feet seemed to turn to Miriam's; on the rare occasions that she was in Miriam's house she turned toward those stairs she had climbed so many times; the one time that she found herself upstairs in that house, she couldn't resist going down to the end of the hall and trying the door to Sister's room. It was locked, and Miriam professed to have lost the key.

So Queenie was left alone in James's house. Because she had always taken her meals either at Elinor's or at Sister's, she didn't even have a cook. She had a girl come in three days a week to clean, and another girl came in twice a week to do laundry, but these weren't Sapps, and Queenie had never grown close to them. Elinor invited her to come and live with them, but Queenie declined: four people in one house was enough, she said. Lucille and Grace offered the permanent hospitality of Gavin Pond Farm, but Queenie turned this down as well: she had never lived in the country, and she was too old to change her ways now. She would have moved next door to Sister's in a minute, but Miriam and Malcolm did not invite her. Queenie even went so far as to suggest such an invitation to her son, but Malcolm replied, "Mama, I have already asked Miriam to ask you, 'cause I miss you, but Miriam says no."

"Why does Miriam say no?"

"She says that you being around the house reminds her too much of Sister. That's why she never even invites you to visit us. Miriam doesn't say much, Mama, but I think she misses Sister pretty bad." With this, Queenie did not argue.

When she was home, which was much of the time, Queenie sat either in her room or on the front porch, waiting for some member of the family to walk by so that she might harness him into inviting her to go elsewhere, or at least into a few minutes' conversation.

Her movements around the house were very circumscribed; she used only her bedroom, the bathroom attached to it, and the front porch. She had established narrow, unvarying routes through the other rooms—it was necessary to go through them to get out the front door, or out the back door—and they were like familiar paths through a forest. One could walk those paths three or four times a day, calm and confident of safety, and never venture off into the dark and dangerous groves that loomed on either side of the needle-strewn track. The kitchen was empty; Queenie had cleared it of all food because she detested roaches. James's rooms, filled with the furniture of James's mother, and all James's things, remained as they were on the night that James died. Queenie had never moved a thing. The extra bedrooms were filling up with boxes of the Caskeys' cast-off clothing, now that the closets at Elinor's and at Miriam's had been filled up. Queenie never had guests; when she occasionally did entertain, she did so at Elinor's, receiving her friends there. Queenie never realized that her patterns were becoming as entrenched as Sister's had been. Because Queenie could get around—though she never went far—those patterns were not so apparent to the casual observer—or to her.

At night, Queenie was frightened. She had never slept in a house alone before, and James's house seemed particularly lonely. The rooms were shadowy, filled with curious shapes and noises. Some small animal had got into the attic and there it scrabbled about all night long. Boards creaked beneath the weight of stacked boxes, and every now and then James's delicate china would rattle in the cupboards as if being moved by an unseen hand. When Queenie had undressed she would look out of her window; she saw nothing but the levee quivering in a shroud of black kudzu, and a corner of the DeBordenave house next door, still boarded over. The wind sometimes picked up sand from the yard and flung it against the house, so that she was awakened with what sounded like infinitesimal raindrops.

Sister had once told her, "Old women don't sleep well." Not having experienced this, Queenie had not then believed it, but now she found that Sister's insomnia had come to her. She would lay long hours awake, seeming never to fall asleep at all. That she did so was proved only by the fact that she awoke in the morning. But how long she had slept, Queenie could never say.

She would lie rigid in her bed, catching every noise in the house and noting it down on a little mental pad, the dimensions of which grew with each succeeding night. Some nights she was troubled with the blowing sand, other nights by the creaking boards, other nights by the rattling crockery. Queenie lay awake and trembling.

Occasionally, new noises came. Something in the house would seem to shake that she had never heard disturbed before. The crystal drops on the candelabra on the dining room table would now and then chime together, as if someone were in that closed-off room, moving restlessly but quietly around and around the table, gently agitating the table and the candelabra with his tread. Or one of the windows opening onto the front porch would shake in its sash as if someone were surreptitiously pacing the porch. Sometimes Queenie thought she could hear the doorknob rattle.

One night she heard the window in its sash, and thought, *it's the wind.* A few minutes later, she heard the rattle of the doorknob, and thought, *It must be a change in the temperature.*

Then she was certain she heard footsteps, light and secretive at first, up and down the length of the porch, then heavier, as if in mockery, as if to say, *And what is the explanation for this, Queenie Strickland?*

She quickly picked up the telephone, but just as she lifted the receiver, the sound of the footsteps stopped.

But the footsteps returned the following night, and again when Queenie lifted the telephone, they stopped. This time, however, as soon as Queenie put down the receiver, the knob of the front door rattled frantically. Then the front door was kicked in its frame, kicked, kicked, and kicked hard, and then the steps, up and down the length of the porch, resumed, loud and angry, strides in boots. Queenie followed the sound from one end of the porch to the other. They shook the house. The glass in the windows shook; the candelabra tinkled together; the crockery shook in all the cabinets; the boxes in the bedrooms surrounding Queenie's slid about; and the small animal raced frenziedly about in the attic.

All at once the noise left off. With a rattle, and the echo of a rattle, the house was still. Queenie huddled in her bed, waiting for the sound of the boots to begin again. All remained quiet.

Then Queenie, still staring in the dark, slowly reached for the telephone. Just as she did so, the closed door into the hallway was suddenly framed with a white soft light, as if a lamp in the front parlor had been turned on. Then the light grew stronger, as if perhaps the chandelier in the dining room had been lighted. Another intensification, this one much greater, led Queenie to believe that the hallway light itself had been flicked on.

Other lights came on in the house, until the doorway was framed in a blinding illumination.

Yet all was quiet.

Queenie, not even thinking, rose from the bed, went to the door into the hallway and opened it. She quickly closed her eyes against the glare. Every light in the house had been turned on. She moved to the switch plate in the hallway, and tried to press the off button—but it was already depressed. She pressed the on button, and the overhead light continued to shine. She pressed the off; still it remained. She went into the living room. Every lamp burned, as did the small cast-iron chandelier overhead. Queenie turned the switch on the nearest lamp, but that made no difference. She hurried to each lamp in the room, frantically turning switches. She jerked a cord from the wall, but all the bulbs shone on.

Queenie ran down the hall and into the kitchen. There too the lights burned, even the bulbs in the closets and the flashlights in the drawers. The bathroom lights, the lights in the bedrooms, the ones in the bedroom closets, in the linen cupboards, on the back porch, in the breakfast room, above the portrait of Grace and Genevieve, behind the closed oven door. The tube of the television set glowed brightly white, but there was no image.

Now the light seemed to grow more intense. Every one of the thousands of objects in that house, illuminated from a dozen directions at once, cast a phantasmagoria of shadows on the walls. The light beat about Queenie and was as suffocating as if she were being rolled in cotton. The light grew so bright and white and harsh that the color seemed to drain from everything around her.

Yet all remained silent.

Queenie stood in the doorway of the dining room, just in the spot where James Caskey had fallen dead, and stared around her in a daze. Her eyes were pained with the brightness.

And the lights grew brighter still.

In the living room, there was a small explosion of glass. Queenie instinctively turned toward the sound.

Then there was a smaller burst from behind her, and then another. She turned and saw the flame-shaped bulbs of the chandelier, each burning with an intensity she had never known before, exploding one by one in tiny showers of glass. The light over the portrait of Grace and Genevieve popped with a kind of wet sizzle, and liquid fragments of melting glass poured down over the painted faces of Queenie's sister and niece.

More explosions began at either end of the hallway, in the parlors at one end and in the kitchen at the other. For a moment the television shone with the brightness of the sun, then suddenly burned as intensely black, and collapsed in on itself with a crash.

Queenie ran back toward her room. The overhead light in the hallway burned more brightly as she drew nearer to it. It began to hum, and Queenie barely managed to get inside her room before the fixture exploded. Shining fragments of glass and metal flew into the room along the plane of the closing door.

In Queenie's room, all remained dark. She leaned against the door, allowing her eyes to adjust to the darkness. She listened to the explosions, less violent now, more widely spaced, but still continuing. The intensity of light appearing beneath the door was less each time Queenie looked down between her feet.

After a while, the explosions halted altogether. No light came beneath the door into the hallway.

Queenie, not knowing what else to do, returned to her bed.

An electrical storm, she said to herself.

She moved to the window and looked out, hoping desperately to see storm clouds overhead. She saw only stars.

The window was open and the night was still, so

Queenie was able to hear the footsteps—heavy booted footsteps crossing the sandy Caskey yards.

She unhooked the window screen and pushed her head out.

There, by the light of the setting moon, she made out the figure of a man striding toward the levee.

He didn't need to turn for Queenie to identify him. She knew him by his stride, and by those boots— boots she herself had purchased.

It was Carl Strickland, her husband, who had been dead these thirty years, drowned in the black waters of the Perdido.

CHAPTER 76

The Caskey Children

"Mama," said Malcolm in amazement, "what the hell were you doing over here last night? Did you get mad at somebody or something?"

With the exception of the ones in Queenie's own room, every light in the house looked as though it had been smashed with a hammer. The fixtures had been shattered, melted, or twisted beyond all further use.

Queenie, following Malcolm around so closely that he bumped into her every time he turned around, said vaguely, "There was some sort of electrical storm last night. Didn't you and Miriam hear it?"

"Didn't hear anything, Mama. You got any idea how long it's gone take me to clean this mess up? Looks like we got to get this whole damn place rewired. Probably never was done right."

"That was it," said Queenie, hastily pinning the blame on faulty wiring and abandoning the electrical storm fantasy. "Bad wiring. Lucky I didn't burn up."

"Mama, you better go out and stay with Grace and Lucille for a few days and let me take care of all this."

To this Queenie readily assented, and that very morning, while Malcolm, still puzzled, waded through the wreckage, she drove out to Gavin Pond Farm.

"Here I am," she cried to Lucille as she squeezed out from behind the steering wheel.

"Mama," said Lucille, "you should have called so Luvadia could have fixed you something special."

"I didn't want to call," said Queenie, rushing forward to hug her daughter. "Because I was afraid you'd tell me to stay away."

"Stay away? Why on earth would we say something like that?"

" 'Cause I've come to stay."

"Well, it's about time, Mama. Grace and I have been asking and asking!"

"Not forever, but for a few days. All the wiring blew in the house last night, and Malcolm told me to come out while he was fixing it."

"Oh, Mama, we're gone have the best time!" cried Lucille, putting her arm around Queenie's waist—or as far around it as her arm would go—and walking slowly toward the house.

Queenie, however, didn't have a very good time. She missed her daily routines in Perdido, as dull as they had been. She missed catching glimpses of Malcolm and Miriam, she missed lunches over at Elinor's. Perdido hadn't seemed much when she lived there, but compared to Gavin Pond Farm, it was the center of the universe. Queenie was particularly lonely at the farm, for Grace and Lucille were busy all day long with everything they had to tend—the camellia garden, the orchards, the cattle, the hogs, and the horses. And for some reason it seemed hotter out in the country than it did in town, and so Queenie sat all morning long in the air conditioned kitchen with Luvadia, watching game shows on television. When Tommy Lee got home in the middle of the afternoon, he kept his grandmother company. One afternoon Tommy Lee got out the shotgun that Elinor had given him the Christmas previous and began to clean it, explaining to Queenie how it was put together and how it worked.

"You remind me of Lucille's daddy," said Queenie, and she didn't say this with pleasure. "Except he was the meanest man ever to walk on the face of the earth, and I don't believe you are."

"No, ma'am," said Tommy Lee, who was fifteen

59

and quiet and shy, even around his grandmother. "I don't believe I am."

Tommy Lee Burgess was on the periphery of the Caskey dominion. He hadn't the Caskey drive, he hadn't their intelligence or sharpness. Though he was strong, he didn't play sports in school. Sports would have interfered with his pleasures at home. He coveted those hours after school, when he had time enough to fish for an hour or so in the pond, or swim in the pool, shoot a pheasant in the woods, or ride a horse around and around the pecan orchard with Grace. He was tolerably well liked at school in Babylon, but had few friends. All his allegiance was to his mother and to Grace. With them—and with them alone—was Tommy Lee ever really at ease. His sole companion his own age was Sammy Sapp, Luvadia's boy, but Sammy spent so much time caddying for Oscar these days that Tommy Lee saw little of him anymore. Tommy Lee was quiet, and a little bumbling, and Lucille and Grace loved him to death.

Queenie had actually never paid much attention to her grandson before. He was too quiet for her taste. Perhaps if he had been ill-behaved, he would have caught more of her attention. But he had never intruded himself upon Queenie's consciousness, and so had been passed over.

She saw more of him during the time that she spent at the farm than she ever had before. School let out for the summer at the beginning of the second week of Queenie's stay, so after that Tommy Lee was around all the time. The boy had just received his driving learner's permit, and since Grace and Lucille were busy as usual, Queenie volunteered to give him lessons. For several hours each day they bumped around the farm in the older pickup truck, and Queenie never once suspected, through all her careful instructions, that Tommy Lee had been driving since he was ten.

* * *

The damage to Queenie's house was so extensive that two full weeks were required to fix it. It might possibly have taken less time if Malcolm had been content with a patch job, but he insisted on doing it right. Both Elinor and Miriam had surveyed the damage to Queenie's house. "It wasn't an electrical storm that did *this*," said Miriam firmly. "And Malcolm, it wasn't bad wiring either." Elinor said nothing, but she helped Malcolm to pick out new lamps in Pensacola.

At last, on the first of June, Malcolm called his mother and told her she might return home. The entire house had been rewired, and if even one single bulb burned out in the next three months, he promised he would sit down at the dinner table and eat it in front of polled witnesses.

But Queenie didn't return to Perdido that night, nor the next. Grace and Lucille were pleased, but they were puzzled. Not even the pleasure she got in giving Tommy Lee his driving lessons was equal to the accustomed pleasures of living in Perdido. When it came down to it, country living was very trying for Queenie.

"Mama, you are pining away out here," said Lucille at dinner one day. "Much as we want you to stay with us, now that the house is all fixed up, maybe you ought to think about going back to town."

"I have thought about it," said Queenie uneasily.

"And?" said Grace.

Queenie dabbed her mouth with her napkin and reached for more peas. She said bravely, "I won't go back...because I'm afraid."

"Afraid of what?" asked Tommy Lee, surprised.

"I'm an old woman," said Queenie, continuing to spoon peas onto her plate, "and I've never lived by myself before. That old house...it's filled with too many memories. Too many people have lived there. Too many people have died there. And I don't think I can stay in it by myself."

"Well, Queenie," said Grace quickly, "you know

you're welcome out here, but I don't think you'd be happy."

Queenie shook her head. "I miss the excitement of town," she admitted. "But Miriam won't have me, Elinor doesn't have the room, and I'm too old to think of moving anywhere else. Besides, James left me that house. He left me everything in it—*his* things, his pretty things that he loved so much. And I owe it to him—I owe *everything* to your daddy, Grace—to stay there and watch over them. I'd never forgive myself if I didn't go back... but I'm so scared."

"I don't understand," said Tommy Lee. "I don't understand what you're scared of."

"I hear things," said Queenie. She smiled, but the smile was pained. "I see lights, Tommy Lee. I know, you think I'm just an old scairdy-cat woman—hearing things that aren't there, seeing things that don't exist. I know they're not there. I know they don't exist. But I still hear them, and I still see them. The night before I came out here, do you know what I saw when I looked out the window in the middle of the night?"

"What?" said Tommy Lee.

"Lucille," said Queenie, turning away from the boy and toward his mother. "I saw your daddy walking right across the yard. Your daddy came up on the front porch of that house and tried to get in. I heard his boots on the porch. He tried to raise the window, but I had it latched. He tried to open the door, but I had it locked. When he couldn't get in, he got mad, and he made all the lights come on and he broke every bulb and every light in the house. There wasn't any electrical storm. The wiring in that house was fine. *Carl Strickland did it.* He's mad 'cause when he drowned in the Perdido I took Ivey's quarters and I threw them in the water and those quarters kept him down."

"Mama," said Lucille softly. "Daddy's dead. Daddy's been dead for thirty years."

"I know," said Queenie. "But don't you think I'd

still know him if I heard him walking up and down on the front porch? Don't you think I'd know him if I saw him? He was walking back toward the levee. He was going back into the Perdido. Those quarters kept him down, I know they did. Oh, Lord, I wish I had 'em back! I wish I had kept 'em in my pocket! If I go back, I know he'll be on the front porch again at night. When I heard the dishes rattle at night, I knew that was Carl, out on the front porch, rocking in a chair—Lucille, you remember how your daddy always used to sit out on the porch at night and rock. But then he gets up, and walks up and down the porch, looking for a way to get in the house. How can I go back?"

Lucille and Grace said nothing.

"Grandmama?" said Tommy Lee.

"What?"

"What if I went with you?"

Queenie considered this.

"I'd feel protected," she said at last. "Carl didn't come when Malcolm was in the house. It was only when Malcolm got married and moved next door."

"Then I'll go back with you. We can leave tonight. I'll drive you back."

Queenie shook her head. "And then tomorrow you'll come back here. Carl will just be waiting for you to go. It won't do any good."

"But what if I stayed?"

"Stayed?" echoed Grace.

Tommy Lee nodded.

Queenie smiled, then reached over and squeezed Tommy Lee's hand. "You're sweet, but you love this boring old farm. I know how you love it."

Tommy Lee shrugged. "I tell you what," he said. "If Mama and Grace will let me, I'll come stay with you till you feel safe again."

"What about your hunting?" said Grace.

"There's woods right up against Elinor's house. I hunted there with Malcolm one time."

"What about fishing?" said his mother.

63

"There's the Perdido. It's about as close as you can get."

"You'd leave us?" said Lucille, shaking her head in disbelief.

"Grandmama needs me," said Tommy Lee.

"That I do," said Queenie. "Would y'all give Tommy Lee up for a while?"

Grace sighed. "Tommy Lee can do what he wants."

Lucille nodded acquiescence. "Are you gone send him back if he causes you any trouble?"

"This boy?" cried Queenie. "Who's he gone give trouble to?"

"He's not yours," Grace said pointedly. "We're not giving him up the way you gave up Danjo."

"I know that," said Queenie. "I just want the loan of him for a while. When I've used him all up, I'll send him back."

"Make sure you do," said Grace sternly. "And what about school in the fall?"

"Lord, Grace," said Queenie, "the boy just got out of school. Don't already be talking about going back!"

Thus Queenie Strickland returned to Perdido with Tommy Lee Burgess. The Caskeys—and the rest of Perdido as well—wondered just what she had done, or said, or given, to pry the boy away from the farm. And they wondered why she wanted him, particularly when she had taken so little note of him before.

Yet, as if to make up for her previous neglect, Queenie couldn't make enough of Tommy Lee that summer. She bought him three new guns to hunt with; she drove him down to Destin and let him pick out the best set of fishing gear and tackle in the store. She bought him boots for the woods, and a boat for the Perdido. She cleared the boxes out of the bedroom next to hers and moved in the biggest, softest bed she could find. She hired a cook just to fix him breakfast in the morning. Most fifteen-year-olds would have been spoiled and overwhelmed by such attention, but Tommy Lee accepted it with astonishing equanimity. He spent his days hunting and fishing, and his evenings with Queenie, watching television or going out to the Starlite Drive-in for double features. Queenie sat in the car, swatting mosquitoes and forever adjusting the volume control on the speaker; Tommy Lee lay on the hood, his head on a pillow against the windshield, watching the summer lightning quite as much as he watched the picture on the screen.

Queenie often asked Tommy Lee if he weren't growing tired of her, if he wouldn't rather be off with some of his friends instead of being chained to a wearisome old woman. Tommy Lee always shrugged and said that he didn't have any friends, and that he never really got tired of Queenie, except when she asked too many questions.

It was at night, after the ten o'clock news or after an evening at the Starlite, that Tommy Lee proved his real worth to his grandmother. For he left the door to his room open, and at any time of the night Queenie could rise, walk into the hallway, and see him there sleeping. Queenie did that often. And Tommy Lee's presence in the house, as his grandmother had predicted, kept Carl away.

The summer passed quickly for both Queenie and Tommy Lee, and soon the time neared for Tommy Lee to go back to school. Grace and Lucille began talking about his returning to Gavin Pond Farm, and Queenie began to speak of the superiority of the Perdido school system over that of the one in Babylon.

"It's up to Tommy Lee," said Grace at last, when it became apparent that a sort of stalemate had been reached.

Tommy Lee decided to remain with his grandmother. He transferred to the high school in Perdido, and all during the fall of 1959 and the winter and spring of 1960, he spent five days a week in Perdido and Saturdays and Sundays at Gavin Pond Farm.

Every night, however, he slept in the bedroom next to Queenie's. Carl Strickland remained at bay.

This development was remarked upon widely in Perdido. Yet another Caskey offspring had been given away. In the whole history of the family, the only child to have remained with its parents was Frances, and Frances was now dead. Lilah, though she lived in the same house as her father, belonged not to him so much as to Elinor. When Frances drowned in the Perdido, Lilah had become her grandmother's child; Billy Bronze became a sort of uncle to his daughter. He took no more part than that in her upbringing. Elinor gave permission, Elinor refused requests, Elinor decided what might or might not be done; Elinor bought Lilah's clothes, and paid for Lilah's pleasures. Billy watched his daughter grow up with affection and interest, but not with the love or involvement of a parent.

Perdido rather hoped that Miriam Caskey Strickland would conceive a child—she was nearing forty, and there wasn't much more time for her—because Perdido wanted to make bets on who would end up with it. Miriam, of all Caskeys within memory, was least likely to want to hold on to a son or a daughter if anyone were to step forward with an offer. The often-heard remark was that if it was a girl, she'd trade it for diamonds; if it was a boy, for oil-company stock.

Perhaps that was what Miriam would have done, had she had a child. But Miriam didn't conceive, though she and Malcolm went at it with the application that Miriam brought to everything. Malcolm had been surprised by his wife's change of heart, and even went so far as to question her about it. "You didn't always want a baby, you know," he pointed out. "You said you'd use its head for a pin-cushion."

"Married people have babies," Miriam replied, a little uncomfortably. "So I changed my mind, that's all. I decided that if I was gone go to the trouble of marrying you—and Malcolm, there never *was* a man who was more trouble than you—then I might as well go on and do the other thing, too." Yet no child came, and it began to look as if no child would.

This irked Miriam. She didn't like being thwarted, and that it was her own body that was proving recalcitrant was a double insult. Malcolm tried to point out to his disappointed wife that a child was only likely to prove a burden to her. Pregnancy itself was likely to interfere with her work; the child would demand time and attention that Miriam would probably resent not giving to the mill and the oil business.

Miriam wasn't consoled. "I could still go to the office if I got pregnant," she said. "And if once in a while I couldn't, I could tell you and Billy what to do and I suppose you would get it done. Once the child came, I'd hire a girl to take care of it." All Zaddie and Ivey's brothers had been long married, and already there was a third generation of female Sapps, just pining to be hired on by the Caskeys. "And if that didn't work out, I could always send it out to Gavin Pond Farm or over to Elinor's. They'd all leap at the chance for another baby. After all, there hasn't been a baby around here since Lilah was born."

But Miriam still didn't conceive, and finally she was convinced by Malcolm and her own body that it would never happen. This didn't, however, lessen her desire to have a child. She looked next door, and saw how Queenie had stolen Tommy Lee away from Lucille and Grace. And when Miriam looked the other way, what she saw was Lilah Bronze, just ripe for the plucking.

Lilah was thirteen, in the eighth grade, and was like no one so much as Miriam herself: starchly handsome, proud of her position, enamored of jewels and worldly things, slightly contemptuous of those her own age. In short, Lilah was a child after her aunt's heart. There was already a certain intimacy between them on account of Miriam's jewelry collection, which Lilah passionately coveted.

Miriam saw no reason why she should not have Lilah for her own. Certainly, following Malcolm's arguments, that would be better than giving birth to a child herself. There was no pregnancy to worry about, no infancy to be endured, and there was not the uncertainty of personality to contend with. She might, after all, have given birth to a child who would turn out to be just like Malcolm—or, worse, like Frances. Just because a woman had carried a child in her womb was no guarantee that she would feel any sympathy with it.

But here was Lilah, and Lilah—to Miriam—was the perfect daughter.

Once she had come to this conclusion, and without having conferred with Malcolm, Miriam lost no time in beginning the task of getting Lilah away from her father and her grandmother.

Christmas of 1960 was held at Gavin Pond Farm in order to celebrate the new facade that had been raised against the old farmhouse, a feature that obliterated the last vestiges of the original humble old house. The house now had high tall windows and a wide front porch with soaring columns and brick flooring. There was a triangular pediment over the double doors. Grace built a new addition every year or so, and by the time that Lucille had succeeded in properly furnishing and decorating the new rooms, Grace was planning the next enlargement.

Now, one whole room was filled with the Christmas tree and gifts, and the Caskeys had to sit on chairs in the hallway and in the dining room in order to open their presents. Most family members gave each of the others about five gifts—even if Elinor had to buy and wrap all of Oscar's presents from him to her, the gifts were still there.

From Miriam to Lilah, however, there was but a single gift, a small box, hidden away near the base of the tree, and this was brought out at the last. Lilah, expecting scarcely anything of consequence from her aunt, who was known for the inappropriateness of her gifts, was astonished to find inside a brooch of diamonds surrounding a ruby that must have been of at least two karats.

"Is this real?" Lilah exclaimed, holding the bauble high in the air for everyone to see. "Miriam," she cried, looking at the tag to make certain that it was indeed from her aunt, "is this real?"

"It is," said Miriam.

"That cost a fortune," exclaimed Queenie. "Or is that just one of yours?"

"I bought it in New York last month," pronounced Miriam. "Especially for Lilah."

"You're too young to wear a thing like that," said Elinor.

"But it's *mine*," said Lilah, closing both hands around it and pressing those closed fists happily against her breast.

"Open a safety-deposit box for yourself," said Miriam. "By the time I was your age, I was already on my second. You've got some catching up to do."

"I am not going to spend good money on jewels for that child that she will never wear," said Elinor pointedly.

Miriam laughed. "You cain't insult me, Elinor. And you cain't stop me from giving Lilah more when I want to."

"No, I can't," said Elinor. "You want to give gifts away like that, go right ahead."

Afterward, at the dinner table, Lilah contrived to sit next to her aunt. "Why did you give me this?" Lilah asked, still clutching the brooch. "I love it."

Miriam answered in a voice that was meant to be heard by all the table, "I gave it to you because I want you to move next door with Malcolm and me."

Lilah's mouth fell open. She turned her head and looked, not to her father, but to her grandmother, seated at the head of the table. Grace and Lucille had happily relinquished their usual places to Elinor and Oscar, as heads of the family.

Elinor said nothing.

"Close your mouth, Lilah," said Grace dryly. "You'll catch flies."

Lilah shut her mouth.

"Malcolm and I are lonesome," said Miriam. "Aren't we, Malcolm?"

"We sure are," said Malcolm obediently from his forgotten corner of the long table.

"You've had Lilah for thirteen years, Elinor. You ought to let me have her for a little while."

"Lilah belongs to Billy," Oscar pointed out from the end of the table opposite his wife.

"Lilah does what she wants," sighed Billy, bowing out. "Or what Elinor wants."

"Lilah," said Queenie, "what do you want?"

"I don't know," said Lilah thoughtfully. "I'd just be moving next door, wouldn't I?"

No one bothered to answer that question.

"Lilah?" said her grandmother. Nothing in Elinor's tone gave the child any clue what she wanted to hear.

"Maybe if I just stayed for a few weeks... until spring vacation or something, so Miriam and Malcolm wouldn't be so lonely. Then I could come back."

The Caskeys all looked at one another, each with complete knowledge. Elinor had allowed Lilah to speak, and Lilah had proclaimed her doom. Caskey children, once given up, were never returned. Lilah Bronze, in that one heedless moment, was lost to Elinor forever.

Miriam smiled, and squeezed Lilah's hand. "Just for a few weeks," said Miriam. "And then I'll let you go back. Elinor won't rent out your room, I guess."

No more was said of the matter at the table. Lilah, who thought herself prodigiously smart, understood nothing at all. The occasion—outside of Lilah's own happiness at the prospect of more jewels—turned not somber, but solemn. Something momentous had

70

happened, altogether unexpectedly, and everybody—except the child who would be most affected by it—knew it. Luvadia and Melva continued to bring out plates of hot rolls and to take away empty dishes, and there was talk still of renewed oil leases and proposed trips to Houston and New York. At one point Oscar sent Sammy out to start the car so that it would be warm by the time he wanted to drive up to the golf course in Brewton, but no one thought of anything but Lilah, who had been stolen away in the twinkling of Miriam's acquisitive eye, more quickly and more cleanly than long-armed gypsies could have done it by reaching in an unlatched window and snatching her sleeping from her cradle.

Oscar didn't wait for coffee; he and Tommy Lee and Sammy drove off to Brewton. Lucille and Queenie went to help Luvadia and Zaddie clean up the mess in the hallway. Grace and Billy started to pack the cars with all the gifts. Elinor remained at the head of the table, with her cold coffee before her. Miriam was on her third cup. She had an arm around Lilah, weary and happy in the chair next to her.

"You didn't fight," said Miriam.

"Fight about what?" asked Lilah.

"Shhh!" said Miriam.

Elinor slowly shook her head.

"Why not?" asked Miriam curiously. "You could have fought. You might even have won."

Elinor paused a long time before answering. One hand was crossed over her breast, the other fingered the black pearls about her neck. "When I gave you Mary-Love's wedding ring..."

"Yes?" said Miriam, holding up the hand that bore the ring.

"It wasn't enough, was it?"

"No," said Miriam, "it wasn't."

"Wasn't enough for *what?*" asked Lilah.

"Be quiet," said Miriam in a slow whisper, pinching Lilah's arm as she did so.

"But now," said Elinor, "we're even."

71

"Yes," returned Miriam. "I guess we are. How's that, Mama? After thirty-nine years, I forgive you."

Elinor said nothing, she just sipped her cold coffee.

For the first time in her entire life, Miriam had called Elinor *Mama*.

CHAPTER 77

The Song of the Shepherdess

Lilah moved into one of the guest bedrooms of Miriam's house later that Christmas day, "just for a few weeks." Only Lilah herself—of all the Caskeys and most of Perdido—was deceived into thinking that she would soon return to her grandmother and her father.

Those few weeks passed, and Lilah said to her grandmother, "Miriam and Malcolm said they cain't do without me. May I stay for just a little while longer?"

"I'll send your things over," said Elinor.

Lilah's clothes went next door, and soon there was no thought whatsoever—even in Lilah's mind—of her returning. She belonged to Miriam and Malcolm now, and though all the Caskeys ate dinner together at Elinor's every evening, and Lilah saw almost as much of Billy as she had before, she was quite a different child. Miriam pampered her niece, oddly, by neglecting her. Elinor had always kept a tight rein on her granddaughter, for Lilah tended to be forward and precocious, protective of her prerogatives as a Caskey and the richest little girl in the entire county; she was apt to be imperious toward the servants. Elinor had kept these tendencies in check. Miriam did not even try to do so. In her niece, Miriam saw the child she had herself been. She trusted Lilah as she trusted herself. What Lilah wanted was what Lilah needed; what Lilah did was exactly what was required by the situation in question. Lilah, in short, grew unbearable. Yet Miriam saw nothing of this, or perhaps she chose to see nothing. For all the child's arrogance, she was still dear to Miriam, and perhaps dearer to Miriam as she became less and less pleasant to others.

Oscar saw all this, and remonstrated with his wife and son-in-law. Elinor and Billy, he said, ought to step in before the child was completely ruined. Elinor and Billy, however, would do nothing. Lilah now belonged to Miriam , and Miriam was raising her as she saw fit.

"It's none of my business anymore," said Billy. "It might be if Lilah still lived here, but she doesn't."

"Oscar," Elinor pointed out, "Miriam is treating Lilah exactly the way Mary-Love treated Miriam. Lilah will be a carbon copy of Miriam. Everybody in town sees that. It probably would have happened anyway. There's nothing that I can do about it—and even if there were, I probably wouldn't do it."

If Lilah was worse off from the move, then Miriam, at all events, was better. She now had someone besides herself to take care of. Malcolm didn't count, for Miriam had managed him for a number of years already, and anyway Malcolm didn't require much managing. Despite Miriam's full days at the mill, she drove Lilah to school every morning, and picked her up after school every afternoon. The two of them shopped together in Pensacola for clothes—and sometimes for jewelry. Miriam took Lilah out of school for five days in February and, dragging Malcolm along for the express purpose of carrying packages, they went to New Orleans for Mardi Gras, and then in Lilah's words, "bought the town out." Miriam, as if she had in truth at last forgiven Elinor for having given her away as a baby nearly forty years before, now regularly called Elinor "Mama" and Oscar "Daddy." Miriam allowed somewhat more familiarity among the households, for it was only she, now, of all the Caskeys, who had the perfect American family—father, mother, and child. Elinor's house, Queenie's house, and Lucille and Grace's farm were all perverted and incomplete reflections of that perfect image. Elinor did not fight her, and Miriam gradually came to look upon herself as the pivot of the family. It was time, in her opinion, that Elinor abdicated.

This assumption of ultimate power in the family tended to make Miriam a bit easier in her manner. A usurper must maintain a cold and unyielding demeanor; a sovereign can afford to be gracious.

About this time, there was another significant change in the Caskeys' way of life, and that had to do with servants. For decades, each of the households had got along with one woman apiece. Because of the sterility of the sandy yards that surrounded the Caskey houses, a single gardener had sufficed for all three. Once again, Miriam was the instrument for the change. When Ivey retired after Sister's death, her niece Melva took her place. Melva was a fine cook, but an indifferent housekeeper. And rather than let Melva go just because she didn't know how to clean rugs properly, Malcolm simply went around to the various Sapps and inquired if there was a girl who *did*. He found one readily, and hired her to do cleaning in the house. Now Miriam had two servants, and that was thought sufficient in a house of only three persons, especially when Miriam was away so much and when so many of the family's meals were taken next door anyway.

Queenie had hired one girl to cook breakfast for Tommy Lee, but this girl went to school directly afterward, and did not return until the late afternoon. Since Tommy Lee also was away in the middle of the day, Queenie hired another girl—a Sapp, of course—who wasn't much good at anything, but who kept her excellent company, and that was really all that Queenie needed. She didn't like to be in the house alone even in the daytime.

Zaddie Sapp was past fifty, but still very capable of keeping Elinor's entire house going; she had done

75

so for thirty years, and always completely to Elinor's satisfaction. However, Elinor now considered that Zaddie had no need to work as hard as she did, so she sent Malcolm back around to the Sapps. Malcolm returned with a girl to help with the cooking, another girl who did nothing but clean, and a boy to run errands.

After Bray's death, Oscar had borrowed various men from the mill to act as his chauffeur, but this was an unsatisfactory arrangement. Oscar declared that he just didn't feel right unless there was a Sapp behind the wheel. Sammy Sapp had his driver's license, but he was still in the eleventh grade over in Babylon. Oscar convinced Sammy that he had no need of graduating from high school, which wasn't a very good school anyway, and promised to pay him more than he would ever get working at the mill. Sammy, already very attached to Mr. Oscar, didn't need much convincing. Oscar got Sammy a uniform, and bought a new Lincoln Continental in Sammy's honor. Oscar, whose eyes were growing dimmer all the time because of cataracts, had Sammy drive him out to San Antonio, where he consulted an esteemed eye specialist; he was told that an operation was dangerous, and might result in permanent blindness. Of this Oscar said nothing to his family. Sammy drove Oscar all over the countryside, through a dozen states, always on the lookout for new and untried golf courses. Sammy acted as Oscar's caddy. The young black man grew adept at description, for Oscar, slouched in the back seat of the Continental, eyes shaded against the sun, now did not even bother to look out the windows.

Out at Gavin Pond Farm, Grace and Lucille still claimed that they got along with just Luvadia and Escue, but the fact was that Luvadia had three teenage children besides Sammy, and those three were in permanent requisition. Moreover, there were field workers who came to the farm every day, and men who maintained the heavy machinery, repaired the fences, filled the oil tanks, and doctored the live-stock. Workers on the oil rigs south of the farm some-times wandered up on some excuse or other, and rarely fewer than a dozen persons sat down to the midday meal at Gavin Pond Farm.

After so many years of appearing only a little above the other inhabitants of Perdido, the Caskeys had gradually put away their conservative coarse linen, and now appeared recklessly resplendent. They bought new cars every year; they flew on airplanes in the first-class compartments. When traveling they put up at the best hotels, and shopped in the most expensive stores. Elinor sent Malcolm down to New Orleans once a month and had him bring up a trunk-load of the finest wines and liquors. Elinor enter-tained businessmen and politicians by the score in the course of a year, and grew so adept at hospitality that she was thought a perfect hostess, because everything was accomplished so effortlessly and with such unconscious grace. Perdido was a small pond indeed, but the Caskeys would have made a very decent showing in a body of water of substantially greater dimensions.

The town might have grown resentful if these changes had not been so unconscious on the part of the Caskeys, if the family's sphere had not enlarged itself so naturally and without their seeming ag-gressively to seek this upward climb. No change was perceived in their demeanor around the town, and they treated no individual differently from before. If the Caskeys gave a party—and they now did enter-tain more frequently than before—then the same people were invited this year that had been invited five years before. Only now Perdido was very likely to meet one, or even both, Alabama senators, not to mention a man from Texas who owned seventeen thousand head of cattle, and a woman who called the First Lady of the United States by her Christian name.

* * *

77 .

Tommy Lee, of all the family, was least affected by all these changes. He remained shy and retiring. When looked for, Tommy Lee was always found in a corner, as far out of the way as possible. His favorite corners were the river, on which he loved to fish; the woods, in which he loved to hunt; and Queenie's bedroom, where he sat and talked to his grandmother for many hours on end. He wasn't looked down upon, by any means, by most of the family, for his function in keeping Queenie occupied and happy was a noble one. Queenie had kept Sister company for many, many years; now Queenie was being repaid for that loyalty through the agency of her grandson. And God knew that Tommy Lee was not good for much else.

But Lilah was embarrassed by Tommy Lee. She wished that she had almost anybody else in the entire county for a cousin. He rendered her self-image imperfect. How sophisticated could she be when such a bumbling troglodyte as Tommy Lee was her only teen-aged relative? He wasn't really her cousin, of course, but only her great-uncle's great-nephew by marriage. Whenever anyone at school referred to Tommy Lee as Lilah's cousin, she attempted to explain this rather complicated relationship, but it never did any good. Next day, Tommy Lee Burgess was again Lilah Bronze's cousin. It wouldn't have been so bad if he weren't already getting fat, just like the Stricklands. Queenie was fat, and Lucille was fat. Malcolm was pretty big, but Miriam kept her husband on the go so much that he didn't have time to eat as much as he wanted. Danjo had sent a photograph of himself and his wife Fred in Germany at Christmas, and he was fat, too. Danjo and Fred had two fat little boys, one of whom was already a graf.

Lilah alternated between spates of badgering Tommy Lee unmercifully and ignoring him completely. When she ignored him completely, he might as well not have existed. She wouldn't speak to him, even when they sat next to each other at the dinner table; her eyes wouldn't focus on him when she turned her head in his direction. When she did take notice of him, it was only to pound him relentlessly with questions she knew he couldn't answer: "Why don't you go on a diet?" "If you won't go on a diet, why don't you try out for football?" "Why don't you ever go out on a date?" "Why don't you ask Queenie if you can drive me down to New Orleans so I can go shopping?"

When Lilah was in the ninth grade—a mere freshman in the high school—Tommy Lee was a graduating senior. He asked her to go with him to the senior prom, but she refused. She would certainly not attend her first school dance on the arm of her cousin! Tommy Lee ended up going alone. Malcolm was a chaperon, and so Tommy Lee sat with his uncle at the side of the room all evening long. Malcolm saw how unhappy Tommy Lee was, and he surreptitiously poured bourbon into the boy's punch.

It was Lilah who convinced Tommy Lee to go to college. "You have *got* to go, Tommy Lee, and that's all there is to it."

Tommy Lee was surprised by Lilah's sudden interest in his future, and secretly suspected that her real motive was to get him out of town. He saw well enough how little Miriam liked having him around, but characteristically, he only admired her for the vehemence of her passion against him. But Tommy Lee still couldn't see the need of college for himself.

"Look, Lilah, I'm not any good at all that business."

"All what business?"

"You know, grades and junk. Besides, Grandmama sort of needs me around here."

"Queenie would like to keep you tied to the foot of her bed, that's what Queenie would like to do with you," snapped Lilah. "And if you let her keep you around here, I will never speak to you again."

79

"Grandmama's been real good to me," Tommy Lee pointed out.

"If you went to college," said Lilah, "you could join a fraternity."

Tommy Lee glanced doubtfully at his cousin. "You sure somebody'd ask me?"

"Sure," said Lilah decisively. "You know why? 'Cause you're rich. They find out about things like that. Rich people always get asked to join fraternities, 'cause they know rich people can pay their dues and buy beer for the parties. And rich people bring their cars to school and own beach houses to give parties in and all that."

"How would people know I'm rich?" asked Tommy Lee, who never carried more than two dollars in his pocket, even when he went to Pensacola.

"They find out. They look up people's names. There's a big book and it tells if people are rich or not. A friend of mine saw one in a fraternity house one time," Lilah went on confidently. "So if you went to college, you could join a fraternity, and then you could invite me to come up to all the parties they have. There's a party every Friday night during football season, and then the rest of the year there's one every other Saturday."

"Would you come?"

"Of course I would come!"

"Where should I go?"

"You mean where should you apply?" asked Lilah, considering the question. "Alabama's got more fraternities, but Auburn is closer."

"I don't care," said Tommy Lee. "Whichever one you say, Lilah." He understood now that his going away to college would serve a double purpose for Lilah. It would get him out of town, where he was merely an embarrassment to her, and it would secure her invitations to fraternity parties. To be able, as a mere high school sophomore, to put in an appearance at one of those much whispered-about orgies of drink and delectably loose behavior, would secure

Lilah instant, exalted, and unapproachable stature among her peers.

"Well, until I learn how to drive, you're gone have to come down here and pick me up on Friday afternoon and then bring me back on Saturday. Since Auburn's closer, you better go to Auburn. After I get my driver's license, then maybe you should transfer to Alabama."

Thus it was that Tommy Lee Burgess decided to apply to Auburn; his application, though late, was accepted.

Grace and Lucille were enormously proud, of course. Tommy Lee was lost to them, that they acknowledged, so the two women took pleasure in the thought of his going away to school and making more of himself than anyone had anticipated.

It was Queenie who was despondent, though she couldn't, in all conscience, deny her grandson permission to attend college. In fact, using all her willpower she refused even subtly to attempt to dissuade him from his plans. She could only moon over him, and buy him more clothes than he could possibly pack in the back of the car. In fact, she bought him a new car, one with a larger trunk for that very purpose. She insisted on going up to Auburn and seeing him installed in a dormitory, though Lilah begged her not to. "Look, Queenie," Lilah said, in as peremptory a tone as Miriam herself might have used, "he's only gone be there for two weeks at the most."

Queenie's heart leaped at this thought. "Do you think so?" she cried. "You mean he'll be so homesick that he'll come right back to Perdido! I never did think Tommy Lee was cut out for college."

"No," said Lilah impatiently. "I mean he'll be moving into a fraternity house. I bet he's Pi Eta. Pi Eta gets all the richest boys. They give a toga party every September. So Tommy Lee will be coming back down to pick me up. He's already promised to invite

81

me. Of course if he pledges Pi Epsilon, they have a Polynesian night. I'd rather go to a Polynesia party than a toga party, but I still bet Tommy Lee goes Pi Eta."

In the last week of August 1961, Tommy Lee and Queenie drove up to Auburn in Tommy Lee's new car. Queenie saw him installed in his dormitory room, and watched with pleasure as Tommy Lee tried, with but little success, to fit his mountain of new clothes into the slim closet and the single low chest of drawers that was allotted him. Tommy Lee's roommate showed up too, and Queenie took them both out to a catfish supper.

Queenie spent the night in the Auburn Hotel, and made Tommy Lee stay with her rather than in his room. The next day, Lucille drove up, and was off-handedly introduced to Tommy Lee's astonished roommate as "my farm mama." Late that afternoon, following a tearful farewell, Lucille drove Queenie back to Perdido, and sat with her on the front porch of James's house until midnight.

"I am so lonesome," Queenie said over and over again, "that I just cain't face going inside, knowing that Tommy Lee isn't gone be there."

"You got to go inside, Mama, 'cause I am about dead, and Grace is out there at the farm waiting up for me."

Queenie sighed, rose from her chair, and allowed Lucille to lead her inside the house.

"I could *kill* Lilah Bronze for sending Tommy Lee away like that. And all Lilah wants is an escort to a party where nobody wears anything but a sheet with a grass skirt on underneath it. She could have worn that around the house here, and nobody in Perdido would have said a word about it. But no," Queenie sighed, "she had to send Tommy Lee away."

"Well, Mama," said Lucille, without much sympathy, "now you know about how Grace and I felt when you took Tommy Lee away from us."

"Did you?" said Queenie vaguely.

"We sure did," said Lucille as she turned to leave.

Queenie listened to her daughter's footsteps as Lucille left the house. She heard the front door shut, heard Lucille's tread across the front porch and down the steps. She heard Lucille move across the yard toward her car parked on the road. Lucille's car started up, and soon the noise of the engine was lost behind the screen of ligustrum to the east.

Queenie didn't even pretend to herself that she wanted to sleep. She wanted only to think of Tommy Lee—to think about the fact that he was up in Auburn, in a cramped little cinder-block room in the freshman dormitory, and not where he ought to be, lying comfortably in the big soft bed in the room adjoining hers; in that dim, safe corner of that old house, in the shadow of the Perdido levee. She lay awake for a long time, thinking of her grandson, remembering with pleasure how many times she had sat at the dining room table and watched him eat his breakfast, how many times they had walked together to Elinor's for supper, how they had played double solitaire in the evening, how they had watched television or the movies at the Starlite Drive-in together, how at least five times every evening they said good-night and kissed each other before laying themselves in their beds. She thought about how every night for three years Tommy Lee had kept Carl Strickland from coming back to that house.

Tommy Lee had protected her, and now Queenie was by herself.

Queenie lay absolutely still, thinking no more of Tommy Lee but only of the fact that she was alone.

She heard, in that stillness, the dishes rattle in the kitchen cupboard. It actually wasn't as much of a rattle as just a little vibration, but Queenie had lived too long in that house not to know when the dishes in the cupboards were disturbed. Down at the other end of the darkened hallway, beyond the dark-

83

stained swinging door, in the closed cupboards, James's best china was shaking with the surreptitious footsteps of someone walking as slowly and softly as he could, up and down on the front porch.

Queenie was suddenly smitten with doubt as to whether or not Lucille had locked the front door on her way out. Queenie got out of bed and crept slowly and softly to the door of her room. She peered out into the hallway toward the front of the house. All was dark, still, and silent.

She stepped out into the hallway, and the crystals on the candelabra on the dining room table chimed softly together. Queenie wasn't afraid of *that*, though, for her own footsteps had caused it.

She now stepped quickly toward the front door. She could see it plainly, its white frame glowing in the dimness of that dark house, the white sheers over its glass inserts shaking almost imperceptibly from her footsteps. She could even see the key in the lock. She could even see the key in the lock turning.

Suddenly the whole house was shaking. Just on the other side of the door someone stood turning the key in the lock and stamping up and down on the porch as hard as he could, first one booted foot and then the other, again and again. The key spun around and around in the lock in a way that keys never turn; it spun quickly and then more quickly, while all the glass and china in the house rattled and chimed in the darkness. One booted foot and then the other continued to stamp up and down on the porch, so that the whole house shook and only Queenie, standing in the open double doors of the dining room, remained still and rooted. That darkened house was filled with music, music of rattling, cracking glass, a shrill tumultuous accompaniment to the tympany of those booted feet on the loosening boards of the front porch. The key still spun around and around, catching light that didn't seem to be anywhere else in the room, and dashing it into Queenie's staring eyes. She dizzily grabbed hold of

84

the doorframe for support. Then Queenie saw the key pop out of the lock, and though it fell on the bare wood floor, Queenie couldn't hear it land for the music was so loud in the house, beating in her ears. All was underlaid with the sound of the Perdido rushing along as the Perdido had never rushed before, or maybe that was only the blood in her head, rushing in pulses to the same beat the boots were making on the porch, and the quaking noise of a thousand pieces of china, and crystal, and porcelain in that darkened house.

A Meissen shepherdess on one end of the dining room mantel and her paramour at the other end bounced up and down to the time of that wild music, and as Queenie stared at the shepherdess with her docile ribboned lamb and at the shepherd with his crook and his pipes, she heard their thin piping music. The shepherd played his pipes and the sheperdess sang a song to the rhythm of the boots on the porch. Queenie listened to that song, and *seemed* to understand the words, and would have caught them for sure had not the Meissen shepherdess and the Meissen shepherd suddenly leaped into the air and fallen down, down past the edge of the mantel, down past the tiles with the painted Holland flowers, down past the polished cold grate, down past the cold ashes, down onto the hard smooth bricks of the hearth. His piping stopped and her song ended; the shepherdess and her paramour were only a little heap of colored porcelain, past song and past repair.

The Sapp girl who had always fixed Tommy Lee's breakfast arrived the next morning out of habit, even though she knew she wouldn't be wanted. She wished she had stayed home. She found Queenie, cold and dead, on the floor in the open doorway of the dining room. Two quarters, each bearing the date 1929, were pressed over her eyes, and the key to the house was stuck in her mouth.

CHAPTER 78

College

Queenie Strickland's will divided her fortune between her daughter, Lucille, her son, Malcolm, and her grandson, Tommy Lee Burgess. The acquisition of all that money, stock, land, and returns in the way of royalties and dividends, made no difference to the three legatees. Lucille had so long rested content with Grace, who had come into riches through her father's will many years before, that she didn't care to do anything at all with her new-gotten wealth. Malcolm merely said, "Miriam, you got anything you want done with this money?" When Miriam said no, Malcolm allowed Billy Bronze to continue to invest it as he saw fit. Malcolm was astonished by the monthly reports he always received from Billy, detailing his own fortune, but in the end it had no meaning for him. Money meant even less to Tommy Lee, who was unhappy at Auburn. He did not like his college courses, he still did not make friends easily, he missed Perdido dreadfully, and he mourned his grandmother sincerely. His roommate found it difficult to believe that Tommy Lee's family had any money at all, since Tommy Lee always seemed to be broke. A glance at one of Billy Bronze's reports, however, convinced the roommate of his error. He had never even heard of anyone who was as rich as Tommy Lee Burgess. He gave Tommy Lee a piece of good advice: "Open a checking account here at Auburn, so you don't have to drive back down to Perdido every time you need a five-dollar bill."

Tommy Lee might have benefited further from his

roommate's advice on other points, but things happened as Lilah had predicted. Tommy was asked to pledge the Auburn chapter of Pi Eta. For Lilah's sake, certainly not for his own, he accepted and moved from the dormitory into the fraternity house. On initiation weekend he was stripped naked, bound hand-to-foot, tossed into the trunk of his own car, and deposited on a sandbar in the Chattahoochee River.

The following Friday, he drove down to Perdido and picked up Lilah. Toga parties were a thing of the past for Pi Eta, and the fraternity's first party had an ante-bellum theme. This was even more to Lilah's liking, for it allowed her to wear some of the jewelry she had amassed.

Lilah went to all the Pi Eta parties that spring, and the following autumn she attended all the Auburn football games, whether at home or away, through the courtesy of Tommy Lee. Perdido thought this all a little forward in only a high school sophomore, but Tommy Lee was her cousin, after all, and Miriam merely said, "I wish I had had Lilah's opportunities when I was her age. I am certainly not gone try to interfere with Lilah's pleasure."

In the summer of 1963 Lilah got her driver's license, and the following fall she simply drove up to Auburn to all the Pi Eta parties. She would not let Tommy Lee come home at all until Thanksgiving, for she did not want to miss anv of her weekends away from Perdido. She was furious that the death of President Kennedy caused the biggest of the Pi Eta parties to be canceled.

It came time, in the spring of 1964, for Lilah herself to apply to college. Tommy Lee assumed that she would want to come to Auburn since she seemed to like the place so much. The rest of the Caskeys, however, knew better than to make any such assumption. It wasn't forgotten that Miriam had not announced her intention of going to school *anywhere* until the very day that she left Perdido. They expected no better treatment from Lilah. And they were right to do so. If Lilah had applied anywhere, she had told no one. Miriam suspected, and even confided to Elinor, "Mama, I think Miriam's planning something." She evidently was, for she extracted promises from Miriam and Malcolm not even to *look* at return addresses on the letters that arrived for her in the mail.

Elinor and Miriam would both have denied that they were growing close, but they were mature women, well-settled into their routines and their identities. Miriam was in her early forties, and Elinor, by anyone's accounting, must have been at least twenty years older. Miriam loved coffee, in fact was almost addicted to it. She would remain at the dinner table long after everyone else had wandered off. Usually Elinor remained with her, with a cup filled with cooling coffee set before her as a pretense that she remained only for that.

"You're going to be lonely when Lilah goes away," Elinor warned her daughter. "You're going to be as lonely as I was when you took her away from me."

"You've gotten over it," Miriam said with a shrug.

"Not entirely," said Elinor. "I still miss her."

Miriam smiled. "Do you want her back?"

"The way she is now?" asked Elinor rhetorically, shaking her head and frowning.

"What do you mean, 'the way she is now'?"

"She used to be a sweet child," said Elinor.

"Lilah was never sweet," said Miriam.

"Neither were you. But at least I could keep Lilah in check when she lived over here. I didn't *always* let her have her own way."

"And I do?" asked Miriam.

"You give her anything she wants. You give her much more than she needs."

"I like giving Lilah things," said Miriam. "I wish Grandmama and Sister had given *me* things when I was her age. Everything I've ever gotten, I've had

88

to get for myself. I've worked hard and I've earned everything I have."

"And Lilah hasn't worked two minutes in her entire life. She's never earned anything."

"Lilah graduated valedictorian of her class. I never saw a girl as smart as Lilah. She could have gone to college two years ago if they would have let her in."

"Lilah never had to work for those grades," said Elinor. "I'll say it again. Lilah never had to work for anything. And I think you've neglected to point something out to her."

"What is that, Mama?" asked Miriam.

Elinor didn't answer right away, but fingered her black pearls with a smile, and seemed to savor the word *Mama*.

"Lilah is the only member of this family who doesn't have anything in her own right."

"What does that mean?" said Miriam.

"That means," explained Elinor, "that everybody else has been left money—and left a lot of money—by somebody or other. Everybody else, even Malcolm and Tommy Lee. They've all got money, and a great deal of it. I've seen Billy's reports every month. And Lilah's the only one of us who doesn't get one."

"Aren't you leaving her anything in your will?" asked Miriam. "She's your granddaughter."

"I'm not telling you what's in my will, Miriam. You're not going to find that out until I'm dead, and I'd advise you not to be impatient. I may be alive for a long time to come."

"Well," said Miriam, "*someone* is going to leave Lilah something. Billy—what about Billy?—who else is Billy gone leave his money to? Or Oscar. Oscar's got plenty. I'm not worried about Lilah. You don't think I'm gone let her go without, do you?"

"No," said Elinor, "I don't. I just think it might be to her advantage if you pointed out that she ought to feel just a *little* gratitude to you for all that you've done for her."

"I'm not looking for thank-yous, Mama. And if I want one, I'll get Lilah to send me a Hallmark card."

"She'll send it if you buy it—and lick the stamp."

Miriam called Zaddie out of the kitchen, and Zaddie, without having to be told, brought out a fresh pot of coffee.

"Mama," said Miriam, "what do you think Lilah's going to do about college?"

"I don't know. Why don't you ask her?"

"It's none of my business," said Miriam. "It's her decision. She knows more than I do about which schools are good and which aren't. I went to school during the war. Everything's so different now."

"You'll be paying for it. You have a right to know."

"Tommy Lee thinks she'll go to Auburn."

Elinor shook her head. "I doubt it. That's only what Tommy Lee thinks she'll do. Anyhow, I don't think you need to worry about where she's going to school. I think you ought to be worried about whether you'll ever see her again once she does go off."

The summer drew to a close, and still Lilah had said nothing. Toward the end of August, Miriam had to go to New York, and as a matter of course, asked if Lilah would like to accompany her. Lilah packed her bags, and she and Miriam and Malcolm left the following day. They stayed four nights at the Plaza. While Miriam attended to business during the day, Lilah led Malcolm a merry round down Fifth and up Madison avenues, shopping for clothes. Malcolm carried the packages and signed the checks, and never ventured a complaint as to how much money Lilah was spending.

On the afternoon of the fourth day, Malcolm, laden with packages, staggered behind Lilah into a restaurant on East 57th Street. When they were seated, and she had ordered him a drink, Malcolm said, "You know, Lilah, there's one thing you've forgotten to buy."

"What's that?"

"A couple of more suitcases to get all this stuff home in."

"I won't have to," said Lilah.

"What do you mean?"

"I mean I'm staying here."

Malcolm looked around the restaurant in perplexity.

"At the Plaza? By yourself?"

"No, Malcolm, not at the Plaza and not by myself. I'm going to school here. At Barnard. That's here in New York. It's the girls' college attached to Columbia. It's a good school. Freshman orientation starts on Monday. I've already gotten my dorm assignment. This," she added, indicating the packages stacked beneath the table, "is my fall wardrobe."

It was a good thing that Malcolm's drink was brought quickly. "Bring him another," said Lilah to the waiter.

Malcolm took a big gulp of his first drink.

"Have you told Miriam?" he asked apprehensively.

"Nobody knows except you."

"Listen, honey," said Malcolm. "Everybody in Perdido is gone be real upset when you don't come back with us. Have you thought of that?"

"I don't have time to go back to Perdido, Malcolm. I told you, freshman orientation is on Monday."

"Hey, I guess you knew about this when you came up here."

"Of course I did. I've known about this for months. I was going to have to come up here this weekend anyway. It was just luck that you and Miriam had to go at the same time."

"But why didn't you say goodbye to everybody when you went away?"

"Because I didn't want everybody slobbering over me," said Lilah. "So don't you start either, Malcolm. Here comes your other drink."

It was Malcolm who told Miriam of Lilah's plans that evening when Miriam got back to the hotel.

Lilah sat on the edge of the bed in the next room waiting to be called in. She was, quickly enough.

"Well," Miriam said curtly, "have you seen your dorm room?"

"No, ma'am," said Lilah. "They don't open until Monday."

"I bet it's a two-by-four. Mine was. Don't you want an apartment?"

"Let me stay in the dorm for a while, then I'll see," said Lilah.

"Are there sororities at Barnard?" Miriam asked.

"No, ma'am. And I don't care. I'm too old for that kind of nonsense."

"Do you want Malcolm and me to wait until Monday and make sure you get in all right?"

"Great God, no!" cried Lilah, who shuddered at the thought of her adoptive parents appearing with her at her first day at college. Then she relented, "Well, stay until Sunday night, and then fly back. Pay the bill here so I can stay until Monday morning, and I'll be fine."

And so it was done. Only Tommy Lee was surprised when Miriam and Malcolm returned from New York without Lilah. It was just about the kind of thing the family expected from the girl. Elinor's dinner table, scarcely recovered from the absence of Queenie, seemed abysmally shrunken.

"Did you ask her," said Oscar at dinner, "if she is ever gone let us see her again?"

"She said we could go up and see her in New York," said Malcolm, "as long as we didn't go to the school. She said she didn't want to introduce us." Malcolm shrugged as if to say, *Isn't that just the way you'd think she'd be?* And everyone at the table nodded, as if he had spoken those words aloud.

"She's going to be homesick way up there," predicted Billy Bronze.

"Lilah?" exclaimed Miriam.

"*You* were," said Elinor quickly, "when *you* went away to school, and you were only fifty miles away in Mobile. Grace said that when she went down there to see you, you had been crying yourself to sleep every night."

"I don't remember that," said Miriam.

"Yes, you do," said Oscar. "I never saw anybody so glad to get home that first Thanksgiving."

"You'd better keep an eye on Lilah," suggested Billy. "You'd better make sure she's happy up there."

"I don't want to always be on her back," said Miriam, shaking her head. "She'd think I was trying to interfere."

"Just make sure you go up to New York as often as you can," said Elinor, ignoring her daughter's reasoning. "Keep an eye on her. Malcolm, you can go up there sometimes on your own. Don't make it seem as if you're going to see her, pretend you're delivering papers or something. Buy her some new clothes."

"She'll like *that*," Malcolm said nodding.

The Caskeys needn't have worried. Lilah got along quite well on her own. She was happy to see Miriam or Malcolm or Billy when any of them was in New York, and once she even went so far as to introduce Miriam to her roommate. She came home at Thanksgiving and Christmas and spring holidays that first year, but spent the summer traveling in Europe. She studiously avoided seeing Danjo, even though his son *was* a graf.

Her second year at Barnard, she moved into an apartment on the East Side, and thereafter Miriam and Malcolm stayed at the Carlysle, only three blocks from Lilah's flat. Her second year she returned to Perdido only for Christmas, and her third year she came home only once—for a weekend in April—and that was because it was Miriam's forty-fifth birthday and Miriam bribed her to come with a double strand of pearls—a sort of birthday present in reverse.

After finishing Auburn, Tommy Lee had returned to Perdido. Miriam had offered him a job at the mill, but instead he went back to Grace and Lucille on Gavin Pond Farm. Grace and Lucille were happy to have him, though rather surprised that he chose to stay with them. "It's so pokey out here," said Lucille. "There's nothing to do. Grace and I thought maybe you'd move up to New York to be around Lilah."

"Lilah doesn't want me," Tommy Lee sighed.

"Some other girl might," said Grace tentatively. Tommy Lee shook his head.

"Good," said Grace decisively. "Men have no business getting married. Men just cause women trouble, that's all they're good for. I love you, Tommy Lee, but you probably wouldn't be any better than most of them."

"No," agreed Tommy Lee, "I probably wouldn't."

Tommy Lee hunted and fished and did what he had done seven years earlier, before he had gone off to live with Queenie in Perdido. He seemed genuinely happy, and to wish for no other sort of life than the one he led, so quietly, so lazily. Once, for lack of anything better to do, he plied one of Grace's boats down into the swamp south of the farm and, losing himself in the maze of waterways and hummocks there, eventually came upon one of the oil rigs. This interested him, and he asked questions of the men working there. When they learned that he was a member of the family who owned this land, the men were quite disposed to humor him. He returned to the swamp the next day and the day after that, and soon he had learned all that there was to know. He was able, eventually, to bring Miriam information that proved of considerable value—information that the oil companies had hoped to keep secret from the Caskeys. Miriam realized then that Tommy Lee might prove an asset to her and to the family after all. She talked to him at some length about the oil business that existed on paper, in ledger books, and in contracts, and Tommy Lee picked this up too without much difficulty. He had, for the reason that nothing better presented itself, majored in business in Auburn.

After this, when Malcolm was indisposed or otherwise occupied, Miriam took Tommy Lee with her to Houston or New Orleans or New York. Grace didn't need any prodding at all to add a wing of offices onto the house for Tommy Lee, and she hired Tommy Lee a couple of Babylon high school girls to help with his increasing paperwork.

Tommy Lee made friends with many of the men who worked the oil rigs, and often in the evenings any number of these men would come up to the house and drink beer, tell stories, and chaff Tommy Lee for having so much money and still wanting to make more. Grace and Lucille wandered in and out of these conclaves with huge pots of boiled shrimp, bowls of potato chips, and cases of cold beer. These were good men, Grace maintained, because they worked hard and had no interest in getting married.

But if Gavin Pond Farm often seemed crowded these days, what with Tommy Lee's new friends and all the various workers on the farm, the Caskey compound in Perdido seemed particularly forlorn. Elinor and Oscar and Billy remained alone in the great house, all three growing old together; next door, Malcolm watched television in the evening, while Miriam sat with her papers all spread out on a wide coffee table before the couch.

Queenie's house remained empty. Gradually, it was being filled with the detritus of the wealthy Caskey existence. Old clothes were packed in boxes and stacked in the rooms. Furniture that was no longer wanted was squeezed into rooms that were already filled. Rolled-up fraying carpets were piled up along the walls. Billy kept all the oldest family records there, in neatly stacked and labeled boxes. The kitchen was crammed with old porch furniture. Queenie's bedroom had more than twenty standing lamps in one corner, each of which was forlornly slated for a repair that would never come. Toys of the few Caskey children were all carefully preserved in Tommy Lee's old room. James's precious gimcracks, which had never been properly stored after his death, slid from their shelves and smashed, one by one. Nobody saw them fall, nobody heard them, but each time anyone went into the house, there was another pile of porcelain, glass, or crockery on the floor. Everything was covered with dust, and rats gnawed away at the corners of closed doors. Not only squirrels, but an entire family of raccoons got into the attic. One of the Sapp girls employed by Miriam wouldn't go near the place because she declared that rattlesnakes bred under the back steps.

One stormy night in 1965, lightning struck one of the water oaks in back of the house, and the top third of the tree broke off and crashed through into what had been James's bedroom. The resulting hole was unsightly, but since it was on the side of the house away from Miriam's, it was just patched over with sheets of steel.

In the winter of 1966, while the Caskeys were all at dinner, James's house caught fire. All Perdido's fire-fighting resources were called out, but the house burned to the ground in less than half an hour. The Caskeys watched it, with the appearance of complete impassivity, from the side porch of Miriam's house as Zaddie passed around dessert and Elinor poured coffee from one of James's best silver urns.

CHAPTER 79

Oscar and Elinor

Oscar was suddenly an old man. The burning of Queenie's house made him so, even though he had thought little of it at the time. He had sat on Miriam's porch, drinking his coffee and calling out hellos to the firemen when Elinor told him which men were there. His only regret had been that so many of the things that had been stored in the house might have done somebody some good if they had only given them away.

"Poor old Queenie!" he sighed. "Poor old James, and Genevieve, and Mama."

Yet he declared that he wasn't sorry to see the house go. It was old, and it was impossible to keep up a house that wasn't lived in. It was a firetrap, and you couldn't walk in the door, Sammy Sapp had told him, without a hundred thousand fleas leaping up out of the carpet onto your clothing. Miriam could hire her a colored man to put in a garden there if she wanted, or they could build a big garage for all their cars. The house wasn't needed, it was bound to have burned down sometime anyway.

After that night, the loneliness of survival seemed to oppress Oscar. He began to miss James, and his mother, and Queenie, with a frequency and intensity that surprised and alarmed him. His sight grew dimmer by the day, and as the real light of the outer world was blocked out, old shadows became visible to him. In moments of stillness in the house, when he was thinking of something else, he heard their voices calling to him. He'd turn off the radio at the end of the ball game, and hear Genevieve Caskey—of all people—calling his name in a distant room. "Come in here!" he'd hear her cry, and he'd almost start out of the chair.

Or he'd dream of his mother, lying motionless in the front-room bed. She'd open her eyes and call to him weakly. And just as he'd get up from the rocker at the foot of that bed, he'd wake up—but still hear Mary-Love's voice, muffled, as from behind the closed door of the front room.

Early every morning Sammy Sapp drove him out to the Lake Pinchona Country Club for a round or two of golf, but Oscar could not see the ball after it left the tee and had but a dim sense of the location of the green. "Where'd it go, Sammy?" he'd ask after every stroke. Regardless of where the ball went, Sammy guided Mr. Oscar nearer to the green, and at an appropriate spot he would drop a golf ball out of his pocket. Oscar vaguely suspected this subterfuge, but knew he could not play the game any other way. When, by ten o'clock, other players started to arrive, Oscar declared that he was tired and asked Sammy to drive him home.

He had a powerful radio in the sitting room upstairs, and sat beside it all afternoon, listening to whatever ball games happened to be on, squinting at the Mobile papers held carefully up to the afternoon sunlight through the western windows. When there was no ball game, he read the papers in silence. He had tried to reconvene his domino group, but his remaining cronies were as blind as he, and they found that at night they often miscounted the spots on the old yellowed ivories.

Billy and Miriam kept him up on the news of the mill and of the oil business, but Oscar listened with only half an ear. He had little interest in that anymore. His only real concern was for Tommy Lee and Lilah: he wanted to know when they were going to find mates. "We need us some great-grandchildren, Elinor," he made no scruples about saying. "We need

98

Tommy Lee and Lilah both to find somebody and settle down. And give us some more babies."

"So we can steal them, you mean," Elinor laughed.

"It's been so long since we had babies around here," said Oscar. "This old house is so dead, and Miriam's isn't any better. Too late for Miriam to have children, I suppose."

"Yes," said Elinor.

"And I don't suppose Billy is ever gone get married again."

"No," said Elinor.

"We're gone be awful lonesome here," said Oscar, "if Tommy Lee and Lilah don't get on with it."

"They're still young, both of them," Elinor pointed out.

"I know, I know, but if they don't hurry up, it's not gone do us any good when they do."

He wouldn't have anything to do with people he hadn't known for many, many years. He knew people only by their voices, and those new voices were unfamiliar and discomforting. He declared that the Sapp girl who did the cleaning for them had no idea in the world how to make up a feather bed, so thereafter Elinor and Zaddie made up Oscar's bed for him, plumping his four feather mattresses in a fashion that was satisfactory to him. In the late afternoon, Sammy would drive Oscar around town in the back of the Continental. Sammy described what he saw on both sides of the street. "Here's Mr. Cailleteau coming out of the drugstore, Mr. Oscar, wave out the left window. And Miz Gully is coming out of the Piggly Wiggly parking lot in their new car, it's a red Chevy. She didn't see us so you don't have to wave..."

Oscar wouldn't come down for guests, and when there was a stranger at the table he always excused himself as soon as possible. Sometimes, declaring himself unfit company, he simply had Zaddie bring his dinner upstairs, and he ate it while listening to the television news. Zaddie sat by him at these times and talked with him so that he'd have company—

and so that if he upset his food or needed something she could take care of it without a fuss.

It was a good thing that Zaddie had so many of the younger Sapp girls under her, for increasingly her time was taken up with Oscar. He wanted her during the day to keep him company, and talk to him. They watched *As the World Turns* together, and made predictions as to what would happen next, and expressed nearly constant disapproval of the evil characters' actions. When the Mobile *Press-Register* arrived about three o'clock, Zaddie read it aloud to him. He still made a pretense of trying to read it himself, but Zaddie invariably snatched it out of his hands, saying, "Mr. Oscar, I'm not gone let you sit there and hog that paper. I want to see what's in it, too. So you just sit back and let me read it out loud. You want the front page or the obituaries first today?"

Together, Oscar and Zaddie followed the whole Alabama civil rights business with all the intensity and interest with which they followed the twelve-thirty soap opera.

"Mr. Wallace," Oscar declared, "is coming down hard on your people. Don't you think you and I better send Sammy up there with a letter or something and ask him to ease up a little bit?"

"You write the letter," said Zaddie, "and I will pay for Sammy's gas."

"Are you looking for equality, Zaddie?" Oscar asked, with a little of his old high-flown courtliness.

"Equality with what, Mr. Oscar? Equality with who?"

"Don't you want to be better paid? Don't you want not to have to pay your poll tax? If all your people voted, Zaddie—if they didn't do anything but register all the Sapps in this town—why you could take over. You could have a colored mayor, and a colored sheriff, and a colored I-don't-know-what-all."

"I guess we could," said Zaddie.

"Then do it. If you did it, *you* could be the mayor,

Zaddie. I'd vote for you. So would Elinor. And Miriam and Malcolm, too. You'd be the first colored female mayor in Alabama, I bet."

"I bet I would," said Zaddie. "But who'd read the paper to you every day?"

"I don't know, Zaddie, I don't know. Maybe you ought not run for office after all. I wouldn't feel right if I didn't hear the obituaries every afternoon. Maybe you ought to give up this idea of politics. But I tell you what: in my will, I'll leave you enough money to start up a campaign and beat Mr. Wallace out of office. I bet you could turn Selma and Sylacauga right-side up again."

In the evenings after supper, Oscar went upstairs to his sitting room, closed the door, and turned on his radio. He listened to ball games in far-off places. Billy and Malcolm would often be next door, watching television together. Miriam and Elinor would be downstairs, lingering at the table. Oscar's relish for company was weakening. There wasn't anyone his own age, of his own generation, except for Elinor. James and Mary-Love were long dead, and he thought of them as dead. That is, he never expected either of those two to walk in the door and demand something of him. But Sister and Queenie were another matter. He frequently found himself straining to catch Queenie's shrill laugh from the screened-in porch, or Sister's loud complaints from next door. He turned up the radio louder at his side, as if its volume—rather than death—prevented him from hearing them when they called.

It was only late at night, when the lights had been turned off and the room lay shrouded in real darkness, not just the darkness of his own dim vision, that Oscar became somewhat his old self again. Only Elinor was happy witness to this small, nightly transformation. Oscar and Elinor talked long into the night, of their family, what Lilah must be doing in New York, how Miriam and Malcolm were getting

101

along, the next round of improvements at Gavin Pond Farm. They talked about the town, how the Piggly Wiggly parking lot was to be enlarged, how a fourth third-grade teacher was going to be needed soon, how they ought perhaps to donate some money to have the town hall clock and bells repaired. They traded gossip. Elinor got hers from all over the white community. The black community news was filtered into Oscar's ear through the willing agency of Zaddie Sapp, mostly during the commercials of *As the World Turns*.

Oscar spoke volubly and without restraint with his wife as they lay in bed together, usually with Oscar on his back and Elinor turned toward him on her side, one arm thrown lightly across his chest. When Oscar grew tired at last, he merely interrupted either his wife or himself with a curt "Good-night, Elinor," and fell immediately asleep.

Only once did Elinor refuse this dismissal, and that was on Christmas night of 1967, after they had all spent the day out at Gavin Pond Farm. "Don't go to sleep yet, Oscar. I want to talk to you."

"I'm tired, Elinor. What's it about?" he asked impatiently.

"Your eyes, Oscar. Your eyes were bothering you today. I could see it."

"Everybody could see it, Elinor," said Oscar after a minute. "They'd have to be as blind as I am *not* to have seen it."

"It's gotten worse, hasn't it?"

"Yes. These things do get worse. They don't get better."

"Oscar, there's no point in snapping at me."

"Then let's not talk about it, Elinor!"

"We have to," said Elinor, squeezing his arm. "Soon you're not going to be able to see at all."

Oscar was silent for several moments, then he said in a low voice. "You remember when Sammy and I drove out to Texas about five years ago, 'cause I said there was all those golf courses out there I hadn't been on yet and I wanted to see them before I died?"

"Yes."

"Well, I didn't go out to there to play golf. They've got *terrible* courses out in Texas, and everybody in the world knows it. So I didn't go out there for that. I went out there to see a doctor, a man at Texas A&M Hospital. And I saw him, and he said I could have the operation, but that there was a pretty good chance that I'd come out of it totally blind. So I hopped in the car, and I said, 'Sammy, let's go home. I'm tired of Texas.' I wasn't deceiving you, Elinor. I just didn't have the heart to tell you."

"Oscar, I knew all this."

"How'd you know?" Oscar asked in surprise.

"Sammy told Zaddie that he had driven you to a hospital while you were in Texas, and I made him remember which hospital it was. So I called them up, and I talked to your doctor and he told me."

"Good," said Oscar. "I didn't like deceiving you."

Elinor hugged him close. "Oscar, I'd like to see the day that you put one over on me."

"Me too, Elinor, me too. Can I go to sleep now?"

"No," said Elinor, drawing back. "I talked to that doctor again last week."

"Why'd you do that?" Oscar asked, now alarmed.

"I told him you were getting worse. He said you should go out and see him again. Things may have changed."

"Things *have* changed. I'm worse. I'm a lot worse than I was five years ago. Elinor, do you have *any* idea how much I dreaded going to see that man, how much it took out of me? I don't think I could go back out there by myself."

"You're not," she assured him. "I'm going with you."

"Would you?"

"Of course, I would. You and Sammy can sit in the front seat, and I'll sit in the back seat with your feather mattresses. Oscar," laughed Elinor, "what

103

on earth do they think at the Hilton when you walk in with one suit bag and a colored man carrying five feather mattresses?"

"They say, 'This way to your suite, Mr. Caskey.' I always get a suite, 'cause then they don't care *what* you do. They're used to crazy old rich people, I guess. Poor old Mama," he sighed.

"Poor old Mama what?"

"What would she think of me now? A crazy old rich man, being carted around the South by Luvadia Sapp's boy in a car filled with mattresses and pillows. Mama wasn't sick a day in her life—not till she died, anyway. What would she think of me, so blind that I'm even afraid to get up out of a chair if somebody else is in the room? Afraid I'll bump into something, and they'll find out I cain't see anything at all."

"That's why you and I are going to Texas," whispered Elinor.

"Don't talk to me about it," pleaded Oscar. "Just set it all up. But don't tell me when it's gone be. Don't tell me you've made an appointment and reserved a suite at the hotel. When it's time to go, just say, 'Oscar, put on your pants, we're going for a ride.' And all the way out to Texas, I'll just pretend we're on our way to Pensacola for supper." He laughed at his own weakness.

"That's just how we'll do it," agreed Elinor. "All right, Oscar, you can go to sleep now. All that unwrapping you did today must have tired you out."

"I made Zaddie sit by me," said Oscar, "so she could tell me what everything was. The only time she didn't have to tell me was when I opened Tommy Lee's present—those damned pajamas he gets me every year. Always the wrong kind. That boy doesn't have the first—" He broke off suddenly.

"What's wrong?" asked Elinor.

"Elinor, you got to promise me something."

"What?"

"Don't ask what. Say you'll promise me."

"I'll promise you. Whatever you want, Oscar. What do you want me to promise?"

"Promise me that you'll let me die before you do," he said. "Promise me that you won't make me live on in this big old house alone. Let me die first. Promise me that."

Elinor pressed her face against his shoulder.

"I promise," she said unhesitatingly, and in such a voice that gave him confidence. "I'll be here to take care of you for as long as you live."

"I couldn't do without you," said Oscar quite matter-of-factly as they lay together there in the dark. "I wouldn't even want to try." Elinor said nothing, but she snuggled closer to her husband. "Why did you come?" he asked.

"Come? Come where?"

"Come here to Perdido," said Oscar thoughtfully. "Mama was always asking that question: 'Why did Elinor come to Perdido?' I always said, 'Mama, I don't care. I'm just glad she did.'"

"Mary-Love wasn't glad," said Elinor dryly.

"No, she wasn't," Oscar admitted readily. "She thought you came on purpose, just to snag me."

"How do you know I didn't?"

"Did you?" he asked with calm curiosity. "Did you hide yourself up in the Osceola for three days—"

"Four days."

"—four days, waiting for Bray and me to come along in that old green boat? Remember that old boat?"

"I do," said Elinor.

"Well, did you? Were you lying in wait for me there, like Mama said you were?"

"Oscar, I never wanted anything in this world besides you," Elinor replied evasively.

"And you wanted to be rich, and you wanted to have a big family so you could be head of it. And you wanted to make everybody dress up for dinner, and you wanted—"

Elinor laughed. "Of course I wanted all those
105

things. What woman in her right mind *wouldn't* want them? But those things wouldn't have meant anything to me if you hadn't been here."

"And when I die?" Oscar asked lightly. "And when you're left alone—'cause remember, you just promised I'd die first—and when those things are all you've got left, are you saying they won't mean anything without me?"

"No," said Elinor. "I'm not saying that. And, Oscar, I certainly don't intend to dress you up in your coffin, see you put down next to Mary-Love, and then drop dead across your grave, either. But when you're dead, those other things will start to fade. I know they will. And when they've faded to nothing, then I'll die, too."

"Fade away..." breathed Oscar softly. "Oh, Lord, Elinor, we're so old!"

"That's what happens here," said Elinor.

"Here?"

"Up on dry land, Oscar..."

"That's right," said Oscar. "Up here on dry land. You still didn't answer my question, though."

"What question?"

"Mama's question. When Bray and I were riding through the flooded streets of this town and we rowed by the Osceola, you were sitting in your room on the edge of the bed. I saw you. You know, Elinor, I cried the day they tore that hotel down. I cried because I remember that Easter Sunday morning when I rescued you out of that corner room. But that's the question: did I rescue you? Or were you just waiting there for me to come along? All this—this house, and the mill, and Gavin Pond Farm, and all these rich, rich relatives we've got, oil wells, and stocks and bonds, and Miriam's forty thousand safety-deposit boxes filled with jewelry, and hot-and-cold-running servants, and you and me lying here in this bed in the dark, Elinor—is this my doing because I rescued you, or is this your doing because you were lying in wait for me like Mama always said you were?"

"Your mama," said Elinor, turning over on her other side, away from Oscar, "always did think that she was right, and that everybody else was wrong. Well, Oscar, sometimes Mary-Love *was* right about things."

CHAPTER 80

Oscar's Pajamas

So, without telling Oscar, Elinor made the appointment with the doctor at Texas A&M Hospital, and one day in February she said to her husband, "Oscar, pull on your pants, we're going for a ride." While Oscar was dressing, Elinor and Zaddie stripped the bed. Sammy Sapp and Malcolm took Oscar's five feather mattresses and his four favorite pillows and somehow fitted them into the trunk and the back seat of the Lincoln Continental, leaving enough room for Elinor to squeeze in the back.

"We're just going to Pensacola for supper," Oscar called out to Miriam and Malcolm, who, as Sammy whispered to him, were standing on the front porch of their house. "But y'all don't wait up."

Every ten miles Oscar turned and asked, "Elinor, are we in Pensacola yet?"

"Not long, Oscar. Sammy, what does that sign say just ahead?"

"'Pensacola. Ten miles.'"

"Be patient, Oscar, we'll be there before you know it."

This obvious game tickled Oscar, and he kept it up at wearisome length all the way to Texas. Elinor had booked the largest suite in the biggest hotel in Houston, and Sammy and three bellboys carried up the mattresses and put them in the place of the regular ones. Elinor made up the bed herself, and informed the maids that she would continue to do so.

Oscar saw the doctor the next day, and the doctor pronounced him worse. An operation was more dangerous now than it would have been years before, the chances of total blindness greater. On the other hand, Oscar was nearly blind now, and the operation could not therefore be regarded as much of a gamble.

"He'll do it," said Elinor, and Oscar nodded reluctant agreement.

The operation was performed a week later. Oscar and Elinor and Sammy meantime remained in the hotel, none of them happy to be away from Perdido for so long. The operation was performed, and Oscar emerged from it totally blind.

The mattresses were put back into the car, and Oscar and Elinor, with Sammy behind the wheel, headed back to Perdido. "That supper in Pensacola disagreed with me, Elinor," was all that Oscar said.

As Elinor led Oscar up the sidewalk to the house, she said to him, "We're not going to keep this a secret, Oscar. You know that."

Oscar nodded. "When people see me fall headlong down the town hall steps, they're just gone *know*."

But things were better for Oscar after that, as it turned out. No vision at all was only a little less than what he had got along with before, and at least now there was no disheartening deterioration. He no longer had to make any pretense about his need for help about the house. He had an excuse not to talk to visitors. All his subterfuges and fictions were laid aside with his thick-lensed eyeglasses; he had need of none now. He didn't come down to dinner at all anymore, but remained in his sitting room with Zaddie for company.

Elinor did not seek to halt Oscar's withdrawal into his own world. A week might pass without his leaving the bedroom or his sitting room. The rest of the house grew unfamiliar to him, and to go through other rooms was as trying an adventure for him as attempting to walk down to the Ben Franklin store without a guide. That suite of rooms at the back of the second floor began to smell of Oscar as Sister's bedroom had smelled of her. On fine days, Zaddie would walk him out to the car, and Sammy would drive him around town and then out to the Lake Pinchona Country Club. Sammy would park the Continental next to the golf course and Oscar would sit very still, smelling the newly mown greens and listening with pleasure to the thwacking of the balls and the intermittent cursing of the players. They'd call out to him as they'd pass by, "Hey, Mr. Caskey, don't you want to get out of that hot car and come join us?"

"Who is that calling to me?" Oscar would cry in return.

"It's Fred Jernigan and Roscoe."

"Fred, Roscoe, sure, I'll come out there, if you boys will promise to play with your eyes shut tight."

"We promise," Fred and Roscoe would always laugh, and then move on to the next hole.

Billy Bronze was of some comfort to Oscar in the evenings, for Billy would listen to the ball games with him. But for the other members of the family, Oscar had little patience. Miriam sometimes came to visit for a few minutes—with Malcolm in tow—and would spill out a little news of the mill. Oscar, however, had lost all interest in the Caskey businesses, and only wanted to know what they heard from Lilah, whether she was married yet, if she was seeing people, or if she was interested in any one particular boy. Grace and Lucille and Tommy Lee came much more rarely to Perdido now that Queenie was dead. When they did come, they all paid a visit of respect to Oscar, but had little to say to him. On one such visit, Oscar turned to Tommy Lee and asked, "Tommy Lee, you got any little girlfriends yet?"

"Don't you speak to him of girlfriends, Oscar," Grace snapped. "We don't want him starting to bring home girls we don't approve of, girls we don't know anything about. When Tommy Lee wants to get married, he'll come and tell his farm mamas that he's ready, and Lucille and I will comb the countryside

110

till we find the right one. Isn't that right, Tommy Lee?"

"That's right, Grace," Tommy Lee agreed passively.

"Tommy Lee can marry when Grace and I are dead," said Lucille complacently. "There's no need for him to think about it before then. Tommy Lee is rich," she added, though it wasn't exactly to the point of argument, "and he can have anybody he wants."

"I don't want anybody," said Tommy Lee. "Except Lilah, maybe."

"Well," said Grace, "if Miriam could marry Malcolm, then Lilah could certainly marry you."

"That's what I thought," said Tommy Lee, who had a fairly accurate image of himself and his capabilities. "And that's what I told her."

"And what did Lilah say?" asked Oscar.

"She said, 'Not in a million years.'"

"Grace, speak to Miriam about this," Oscar suggested. "Maybe Miriam could talk some sense into that girl. Tommy Lee, if you and Lilah got married this year, you could start having children before I die."

"I sure would like to oblige you, Oscar," said Tommy Lee.

"I'd rather you gave me a little baby for Christmas than those damned old pajamas."

Zaddie, who had been sitting silently by throughout this little audience, indicated by a motion of her hand that Oscar was weary. Grace, Lucille, and Tommy Lee stood up at that moment, and with only perfunctory ceremony, took their leave.

The winter of 1968 was particularly cold and wet in south Alabama. Everyone suffered through days of freezing rain, high winds, and cloudy chill evenings, imagining that the next day would dawn clear and warm. It rarely did. Out at Gavin Pond Farm, Lucille was worried about some new, small, and very rare camellias she had just set out in the fall. She

111

looked at them carefully every day, and every day grew glummer and glummer, for the expensive plants looked as though they were dying. She went out in the rain every day, shoveled new soil around their roots, carefully covered them with plastic, and constructed small protective fences about them. Toward the end of February, when warmer weather was *sure* to come at last, Lucille's efforts proved a success, and the rare camellias gave every indication of survival. Lucille, however, was now laid up in bed with what seemed to be a severe cold. This, after hanging on for a week, was diagnosed as pneumonia, and she was placed in Sacred Heart Hospital in Pensacola. Grace, Tommy Lee, and Elinor worked out a schedule to spend alternate days with her so that she would never lack for company.

Oscar complained to Elinor about being left alone. "Let Grace or Tommy Lee go. I need you here, Elinor."

"Grace has a lot to do at the farm, Oscar. And Tommy Lee has plenty to keep him busy. I'm glad to go, and I have to do it. Lucille would fret if there wasn't somebody by her bedside. And I don't know what you mean by being all alone anyway. Isn't Zaddie in here every minute of the day when I'm not? Besides, they shoo us out of that hospital at eleven, so I can be home at midnight."

Visiting hours were over much earlier in much of the hospital, but Lucille had a private room, and in any case the Caskeys were a well-known family in the area. There was no trouble made about these quiet visits beyond the stated times.

On these evenings when Elinor was away at Lucille's bedside, Oscar was at a loss. Football season was over, and he was no aficionado of basketball, and so the radio was of no use to him. He pouted at being alone. He'd tell Miriam and Malcolm and Billy to go out somewhere and eat. If Elinor wasn't going to be around, he didn't want any of them. Zaddie brought up his dinner, and then sat with him through

112

the evening news, but directly afterward Oscar sent her down with the tray. "Come back up and turn down my bed, Zaddie. I've got weary bones today."

"It's the rain, Mr. Oscar," said Zaddie comfortingly. "It's the rain makes you tired all the time."

"Maybe. Maybe it is," said Oscar, listening for a moment to the sound of the rain beating against the sill of the sitting room window. "Where'd they go out to dinner? You know?"

"They all went out to the farm, Mr. Oscar. Tommy Lee shot some birds, I guess."

"Not hunting season, though. That's boy's gone get in trouble one of these days. So they've left us all alone, Zaddie."

Zaddie did not go downstairs with the tray, for Oscar seemed disposed to talk. She went into the bedroom and turned his bed down as he liked it.

"That was a good supper, Zaddie!" he called out.

"Glad you liked it," Zaddie called back.

"Just you and me here tonight, Zaddie. You and me and the rain."

"Yes, sir."

"Elinor tells me the rain has beat down all the azaleas this year."

"Yes, sir. Not much left."

"That's too bad. Elinor's always been proud of her azaleas."

Zaddie came back into the sitting room. "You going right to bed, Mr. Oscar?"

"I think I will. All this rain is making me sleepy."

"Me too, Mr. Oscar. You need any help in getting in your pajamas?"

"No, I'll be all right. You go on downstairs. You got a little Sapp down there to help you clean up?"

"I sure do. I got two of them sitting there in the kitchen watching the television."

"All right. I tell you what, Zaddie. You go on down there and get things cleaned up, then come on back up here and just check and make sure I'm all right."

113

Oscar didn't want Zaddie's help in getting undressed —that would have been humiliating. On the other hand, he almost always now needed Elinor's help to untie his shoes, unbuckle his belt, and find the pajamas he liked best. He wasn't so certain that he could manage all that by himself.

"You need the light, Mr. Oscar?" Zaddie asked as she picked up the tray.

"Light's not gone do me much good, Zaddie," Oscar replied in a low, weary voice. "You go on downstairs."

"I'll be back up in a little while and make sure you're comfortable, Mr. Oscar."

Zaddie went downstairs, leaving Oscar in the darkness of the second floor. The rain had increased in intensity in the past half hour. Feeling his way from the sitting room into the bedroom, he passed by the window and was splashed with water. He jerked his arm away, then squeezed his wet sleeve around his wrist. He seated himself on the edge of the bed, and pulled his shoes off without bothering to untie them. He removed his socks, and then went carefully to work on his belt. After a few moments, he was relieved to hear it unbuckle. He removed his pants and his undershorts, then undid the cuffs of his shirt, allowing the links to drop to the floor. He took off his shirt and his undershirt and then shuffled to the dresser. He opened one drawer and felt about for his underwear; but that drawer seemed to have nothing but socks. He opened the drawer below that, and found a pair of pajamas. He put them on, but something about their feel and their odor convinced him that this was not one of the two pairs that he was most used to. He went by slow steps back to the bed and climbed in, pulling the covers up to his chin. Had it not been for the unfamiliar pajamas, he would have been very content. Elinor had made the bed that morning just the way he liked it; Zaddie had turned it down, fixing the pillows just as he always wanted them.

It was still early in the evening, but because the

noise of the rain kept him from hearing—as he might have heard—Zaddie and the young Sapp girls in the kitchen, it seemed very late. Oscar felt that he could have fallen asleep immediately, had it not been for the unfamiliar pajamas. These were probably a pair that Tommy Lee had given him the Christmas before. Tommy Lee, Oscar reflected yet once again, always gave him pajamas, and always the wrong kind. He wondered how many pairs of his wrong kind of pajamas had burned up in James's house. Hundreds, probably. Dressersful, trunksful of pajamas, still in their cellophane packages, still bearing shreds of paper and tape and ribbon.

But not even the feel of the unfamiliar, wrong sort of pajamas was enough to overcome the soporific influence of the beating rain, and Oscar Caskey soon fell deeply asleep.

He awoke sometime later—how much later, he had no way of knowing. It was still raining. The house still felt empty; Elinor was not yet in bed beside him. He sighed, and now wished he hadn't gone to bed so early. He wondered if Zaddie had come back upstairs to check on him. He wished he knew what time it was. One of the problems about being blind was that you never knew what time it was. You lost your ability to gauge passing hours by changes in shadow and light. And now the pajamas felt more uncomfortable than before. Pajamas ought to be made out of cotton, pure cotton, and nothing else, Oscar thought. These were obviously something else; they would keep him awake all night. The more he thought about the pajamas, the more convinced Oscar became that he would have to get up out of bed and find one of the right pairs. Ones that were all cotton, that hadn't been starched, that had been worn in this bed before. While he lay in the bed wondering whether he should get up that very moment or wait for a little bit, he began to think that he heard voices underneath the rain. Perhaps Elinor had returned, and was talking to Zaddie downstairs. The sound of the rain was loud, however, and he couldn't even be certain that his ears weren't playing tricks on him.

"Elinor!" he called. His own voice sounded muffled and dim in the heavy atmosphere. She wouldn't have heard him even if she had been in the next room. "Elinor!" he called again, this time more loudly.

A voice seemed to answer in reply. But whose voice, and where it came from and what it said, he couldn't determine. It was the rain, beating against the sills, foaming down the screens, spilling onto the baseboards, that prevented his knowing who else was in the house.

He lay still, forgetting about the pajamas, and listened, straining to hear a repetition of those voices. His eyes were wide open and staring, but he saw nothing at all.

Oscar!

He heard that. He heard his name called. Whoever had called him was on the second floor, not in the sitting room, but out in the hall. Down the hall, probably all the way at the other end in the front room.

"Elinor?" he said feebly, knowing it was not Elinor, and not Zaddie, who had called to him.

The voice did not come again. Oscar tried to remember it, tried to recreate in his mind, over the noise of the rain, the precise configuration of those two familiar syllables so that he could know who was calling him from the front room. *Billy,* he thought at first. Billy could have gone down the linen corridor from his room to the front room, opened the door, and called his name. Yet it wasn't Billy's voice. Billy said his name differently.

"Who is it?" Oscar called, and pushed back the covers on the bed.

It might have been Miriam, or Malcolm, or even Grace, Oscar thought feverishly—but what would any of them be doing in the front room? No one went up the front part of the house anymore. Wasn't it

116

strange how patterns become ingrained in a reduced household? There were three bedrooms up there, at the front of the house, and they were never used. Oscar had even heard Zaddie say she didn't make up the beds there anymore, because if she did the sheets would get moldy before anybody slept on them again.

Oscar eased down off the bed. The floor was cold, and felt damp beneath his bare feet. He took a few steps toward the door to the sitting rooms, stopping suddenly when he trod painfully on one of his cuff links. He kicked it aside, and went on, waving his arms before him. The air was chill; Zaddie ought to have closed more of the windows, he thought. When he had felt his way to the door he paused, grasping the frame on both sides; he bent forward and listened. He heard nothing but the rain. Though there was but a single window in the sitting room, the noise of the rain seemed louder than it was in the bedroom. If he shut all the windows, he'd be able to hear if his name was called again, but he mistrusted his ability to maneuver that well without stumbling over the furniture. And as long as he was this far, he might as well go out into the hallway.

He did so, and listened intently. The rain drummed against the staircase window to his left. Beneath that drumming, Oscar thought he detected something more—a shuffling, a moving about, and a whispering. It seemed to come from the front of the house—from the front room.

"Elinor?" he called, not because he thought Elinor was in the house, but because it was Elinor who he wished were at his side. He crossed the hallway, and dragging his hand along the damp wallpaper, he made his way toward the front of the house. The whispers and the shuffling stopped, and all he heard was the drumming rain.

"Who is it?" he asked loudly. "Who's in there?"

He reached the front room door and then pressed his ear against one of the panels. A gust of wind blew

117

rain against the door inset with stained glass at the front of the hall, but after a moment, the regular beat of the rain resumed.

Oscar knocked on the front room door. "Who's in there?" he called.

He heard rustling inside, as if someone—or more than just one person—had suddenly moved about.

"Who is it?" he cried again. He pressed his right hand against the door, and ran it downward until he had grasped the knob. He turned the knob, and was about to push the door open, when once more his name was called.

Oscar!

"Mama?" he said. "Mama, is that you?"

He pushed open the door.

"Mama?" he said again.

Oscar!

Him? Is it him? cried the second voice, in an eager piping lisp; the voice of a small boy.

He had heard his mother's voice on his right. Oscar shuffled in that direction. Having no memory of the arrangement of furniture in the front room, he was wary of bumping into something. "Mama, if that's you, answer me." He heard the springs of the bed creak, as if someone had sat down on the edge of it. More creaks, and in different configurations, suggested that someone else had just lain down on the bed.

Him? Is it him? the small voice repeated.

Yes, came the reply from the bed.

Then Oscar heard a slight scuffle against the floor, and then immediately felt small arms—the arms of a child—grasping him around his thighs. The child's arms were wet, and their dampness penetrated the cloth of Oscar's pajamas. Oscar struggled to maintain his balance, but fell forward. Fortunately he was near the bed, and that stopped him. He reached out into that blackness, and his hand was suddenly gripped tight. The hand that grasped his was wet and slick. Its nails dug into his palm.

118

At the same time, the child dragged at his legs, attempting to pull him down to the floor.

This one. This one, hissed the child.

Oscar struggled. He freed his hand, then turned around, sitting on the edge of the bed. He flailed his arms before him, and grabbed the child. The boy tore viciously at Oscar with his long nails.

"Who is this?" Oscar cried, holding the child tight, and drawing him close. The boy was wet all over, and he stank. The foul air of the Perdido was breathed into Oscar's face.

John Robert, said the voice behind Oscar. Oscar felt the mattresses of the bed shifting beneath him. Whoever was behind him was sitting up. Two arms grasped him tightly from behind.

"John Robert DeBordenave," whispered Oscar, suddenly letting the child go. The name came to him without his searching for it, without his even remembering that such a child had ever existed, without his being able to recall what had ever become of him. Oscar heard the boy scramble away. Some small piece of furniture was knocked over, and Oscar heard the splinter of wood.

John Robert was dead. He had drowned in the Perdido. Oscar now remembered that. But if John Robert was dead, and were yet here in this room, then Oscar's mother Mary-Love, who was also dead, might be here as well. Oscar grasped the arms that held him tight. He turned his head over his shoulder. "Mama?" he asked. "Mama, is that you? Don't hold me so tight, you're squeezing me."

But if it was Mary-Love, then Mary-Love wouldn't let go. She squeezed Oscar tighter, until it seemed that he could not breathe at all. And meanwhile John Robert was further smashing up the piece of furniture he had overturned.

The rain beat against the front room windows, and it seemed to Oscar as if he were beneath the waters of the river, so deep and pervasive was the smell of the Perdido in the room. He scarcely noticed

119

at first when John Robert began to beat him about the legs with a stick. But that insensitivity became pain as John Robert turned the stick around and a protruding nail—bent and rusted, but still sharp— was jabbed repeatedly into his legs, ripping his flesh as easily as it ripped the cloth of his pajamas.

"Mama," Oscar pleaded, "stop him. Stop him. I cain't. I'm blind. Mama..."

Oscar may have been wrong. It may not have been Mary-Love. But whoever it was, she did not stop John Robert, but instead she pushed Oscar forward onto the floor. And John Robert stood over him, and beat him about the breast and shoulders with the stick, digging the single nail again and again into Oscar's flesh with a savage monotony.

Oscar lay trembling, and then he lay still. Then he heard his mother's voice, slow and melancholy. *Not for you, Oscar. But for Elinor.*

"Mama?" said Oscar weakly. "Mama, I lost my eyes..."

The relentlessly beating stick moved upward toward Oscar's face.

The eyes, Mary-Love's voice echoed. *John Robert, the eyes*.

"Mama—" Oscar said. It was his last word. John Robert DeBordenave swung the table leg one more time, and that single nail exploded through the cataract of Oscar's eye, burst the eyeball, tore apart the optic nerve, and plunged three inches deep into his brain.

CHAPTER 81

Footsteps

It was Elinor who discovered Oscar's corpse, counted the punctures in his body, extracted the nail that was lodged in his brain, and persuaded Leo Benquith, in senile retirement, to sign a death certificate without even looking at his old friend. It was Elinor who prepared the body for burial, and she and Zaddie who lifted Oscar's stiffened form into his coffin. The town protested loudly, but Elinor said, "Oscar made me promise to do it all myself." The other members of the family did not protest; Elinor had her reasons, doubtlessly, and it was probably best not to enquire into them too closely.

All the furniture in that bedroom and sitting room—the furniture with which Oscar and Elinor had started out their marriage—Elinor gave to Escue Wells and Luvadia Sapp out at Gavin Pond Farm. All Oscar's clothing and the very linen they had used in those rooms was distributed among the poor through the Methodist Church in Baptist Bottom. "These rooms smell of Oscar," Elinor said to Zaddie. "I won't have these rooms smelling of him when I go to sleep at night. I won't be reminded of him like that. I think of him enough as it is."

A rumor got around that Oscar's death had not been natural after all. Murder, however, seemed unlikely. Nobody was at the house that night but Zaddie, and Zaddie's care for Oscar in his blindness was widely known and universally commended. Her lifelong loyalty to the family placed her above suspicion. Since Leo Benquith would not speak, even to provide details that would have corroborated heart failure as the cause of death—as the death certificate read—the town eventually decided that Oscar, depressed because of the failure of the operation on his cataracts, had committed suicide. His last note to Elinor, it was said, was now in a safety-deposit box in Mobile. Suicide was a sufficient explanation for all the mystery surrounding the very private disposition of Oscar Caskey's corpse.

Oscar had withdrawn so from the family the last years of his life that his death made a difference only to Elinor, and Zaddie, and Sammy Sapp, really. Only they had had anything to do with him for the past two years. Poor Sammy Sapp wondered if he'd have to give up his uniform and move back out to the farm. Like so many Sapps before him, he really did prefer the town existence. Elinor kept Sammy on; she said it befitted her station to have a chauffeur.

Perdido watched Elinor closely. The behavior of a widow was always a matter of interest and comment, and Elinor Caskey was, in herself, no ordinary woman. Perdido noticed a number of things: the first was that she did not weep at the funeral. And after that ceremony, she did not wear black, nor did she in any other manner appear to change the routine of her former existence. She went on living just as she had lived when her husband was alive. For the nearly fifty years of their marriage, she had appeared devoted to him, and he to her. Perdido uncharitably concluded that the marriage, in the last years particularly, had been only a sham. Elinor and Oscar had remained together out of convenience, because a rupture would have proved financially inconvenient to the entire family. Elinor and Oscar, Perdido was certain, had grown cold to one another as they got older. Elinor had become exasperated with her husband's blindness, Oscar had shrunk beneath Elinor's lack of sympathy.

In company, even within the family, Elinor never

talked of Oscar. She never made a mistake, as many people do who have lost a loved one, and spoke of him as if he were still alive. Every morning, after the beds had been made, Sammy drove Elinor and Zaddie over to the cemetery and Zaddie got out of the car and placed fresh flowers on Oscar's grave. There was something so cold and perfunctory in this ritual—Elinor never got out of the car; never even rolled down the window, for that matter—that Perdido concluded that it was as false as Elinor's grief. In the new part of town, among the people who had lived in Perdido for only twenty or thirty years, rumor had it that old man Caskey hadn't died a natural death, and that Elinor and her maid had done him in for the money that was to come to both of them.

It was indicative of the changes in the Caskey family that this rumor was able to get started at all; and it was indicative of the changes in the family's relationship to the town that the Caskeys never even got wind of it. Perdido had grown, and Perdido had got rich. The people who had bought up land after the discovery of oil were now rolling in money. And there were the owners of the new shops and other businesses who catered to and serviced this new wealth. The money that spewed up out of the earth, out of hundreds and hundreds of wells, settled over Perdido, and was spouted up again and again, until it seemed that the whole town might drown in it.

The Caskey mill continued, and expanded even further, under Miriam's direction, but it wasn't the small local operation that it had been. Workers now came from all over; they drove down every morning from Brewton, over from Jay, and up from Bay Minette. Three full shifts kept the mills going twenty-four hours a day; Miriam allowed the plants to shut down only on Sundays and national holidays. Of course a great number of people from Perdido still worked at the mill, or made their livings indirectly from it, but it no longer seemed essential to the town's well-being. Perdido now was always full of strangers, people who had no real interest in the town.

The Caskeys, of course, were very rich—far richer than anyone in Perdido suspected, in fact, for they didn't make an ostentatious show of their wealth. The newest house in the Caskey compound was Elinor's, and that had been built fifty years before. All the new wealth in Perdido had put up huge houses on the outskirts of town, with triple-car garages, swimming pools, and tennis courts serving as proof of substantial means. One of the doctors in town even bought himself an airplane, and built a landing strip right beside his house on which to show it off. New wealth constructed beach houses down at Destin, and made yearly trips to Disneyland and Acapulco. New wealth ate out in Pensacola nearly every night, and sent its boys off to military schools in North Carolina and Virginia. Its girls stayed at home and got three years of braces. The Caskeys, however, lived on in their dowdy houses, with their old furniture, and did what they had always done. It was commonly recognized that the Caskeys had allowed Perdido to pass them by.

Queenie's death had broken up the Monday afternoon bridge club, and Elinor did not apparently care to play with the younger women who had taken it over. After Oscar's death Elinor allowed their membership in the Lake Pinchona Country Club to lapse, but an even more drastic change was the fact that the Caskeys no longer went to church. First Elinor stopped going, and then Billy stayed home—to keep her company, he said. Miriam bluntly announced, "Well, Mama, if you can stay away, then I can too. One less time to dress up every week is fine with me. And there is plenty of work I can do." Malcolm would never have thought of doing anything that Miriam didn't do herself, so all the Perdido Caskeys remained away. Elinor still punctually paid a yearly pledge to the church, and, discreetly, she was never to be seen on her front porch or riding around the town during the hours of Sunday school or morning services. The Caskeys' apparent apostasy was much discussed around town, and Perdido postulated decades of arguments between Elinor and Oscar on the subject of church attendance.

With ever greater frequency, Miriam and Malcolm were out of town on business. In the past decade Miriam had found a series of managers who pleased her and to whom she had turned over most of the day-to-day business of the mill. She retained for herself all the more complex, personal, and exciting business of investments and large-scale bargaining. There had been a time when she had relied a great deal on Billy Bronze. When Miriam encountered executives who didn't fancy dealing with a woman, Billy had been there to back her up. But now Miriam herself was well known, and even when she wasn't, she had developed enough finesse to handle just about any situation. Also, on those occasions when she ran into an executive who just *wouldn't* take her seriously because she was a woman, Miriam merely shrugged and walked out in the midst of the conversation, leaving the man to discover later what a foolish mistake he had made. She was rich enough to do that now. Miriam preferred to work alone, and Billy preferred to remain with Elinor. Billy gave up his downtown office, and converted two of the bedrooms upstairs to his own use.

When he was young, Billy Bronze had dreamed of many types of existence, but never this. He would never have chosen Perdido as a place to live. He was certain he didn't like small towns; he always preferred places like Houston and New Orleans. He didn't like the smell of the river. He had no friends in Perdido.

Yet here he was, living in an old house with an aging mother-in-law, rising at seven, sitting down to a formal breakfast in the dining room, and then retiring to his air conditioned office on the second floor, where he looked over the morning mail and talked on the telephone to Miriam at the mill, to brokers in New York, and to oilmen in Texas. He had a secretary come in at noon to type up all his letters, and while she worked Billy had lunch with Elinor and Miriam and Malcolm. After lunch he and Elinor sat out on the screened-in porch and talked until the secretary was finished. Then Billy went back and shut himself in his office again. He most often took supper alone with Elinor in quiet contented splendor. In the evening he watched television, or listened to the ball games on Oscar's radio— the only item of Oscar's private possessions that remained in the house. Billy went to bed early, not because the day had wearied him, but rather because there seemed nothing else to do.

He was quite rich now, richer than he had ever imagined possible; he had inherited all of Frances's money, all his father's, and he had much that he had made himself—but he did nothing at all with it. He never went anywhere, he never bought anything. It was Elinor who said, "Billy, it's about time you had a new suit." And then Sammy Sapp would drive him and Elinor down to Mobile and Elinor would choose three or four new suits for him and pay for them herself. Billy had assumed, when he was young, that he would have a family: a wife and three children— two boys and a girl. He *had* married, of course, but his wife was dead, and he lived on with his widowed mother-in-law. He had had a daughter, but that daughter had been taken away from him. Lilah no longer even called him "Daddy," and he saw her not more than once a year, and only then when it pleased her to come home for Christmas.

All his little dreams as a young man—all those things he would get, and have, and be—were merely means to the end, and the end was personal happiness. Things hadn't turned out the way he imagined they would, not at all, but he was, nonetheless, quite happy. He worried that he was fooling himself, that he was closing his eyes and declaring loudly that the

126

bars that constrained him were not there at all. Perhaps they were there: were this house, and Elinor, and the pecan orchard across the way, and the levee and the river flowing behind the levee, Miriam making demands on him over the telephone on one side, and the dark pine forest on the other. If they were, though, he didn't feel them. He honestly didn't *feel* constrained; or if he did, then it was constraint itself that gave him pleasure.

Now it seemed likely that he would attend Elinor on her death-bed, for he was only forty-seven, and Elinor at this time was probably seventy-four or seventy-five. Sometimes *that* was his thought, and no other, when he raised his eyes from the foot of the dining room table and stared down the expanse of white linen to where his mother-in-law sat, erect and regal, with the candlelight gleaming on the ropes of black pearls about her neck.

Some years before, Oscar had had the house air conditioned throughout, and the two large units, located just under the window of Zaddie's room, hummed loudly from April through October. Oscar had liked the house chilled, for he was very warm-blooded, and Elinor and Billy and Zaddie had grown so used to it that they did not raise the thermostat after Oscar's death. As a result, Billy always slept under covers, and in the summer he always fell asleep with the noise of forced cold air in his ears. That and the hum of the cooling units themselves outside covered up all the small night noises in that large old house—or almost all. As he lay awake so many nights, Billy noticed that his hearing became acuter. He could make out noises *beneath* the air conditioning: the creaks, and the false footpads, the snaps in the furniture, and the slight ringing in cupboards filled with glassware.

Yet the noises on some nights were more than that, more than the occasional creak, snap, and ringing. Sometimes Billy seemed to hear one of the outside doors swinging damply open, as if Zaddie had peered out the back door perhaps to see if the moon had yet risen, and then allowed the door to swing softly shut again. On other nights he seemed to hear footsteps on the stairs. He knew that one stair in particular creaked, on the right-hand side going up, and sometimes he heard that stair. Perhaps Zaddie was going up to the staircase window to peer out at the stars. Billy never got up to look. Once he was in bed, he stayed there. Even when he had nightmares, and lay sweating and trembling in bed, his feet remained unswervingly pointed at the bouquet of violets painted on the foot board and his hands lay palm upward atop the neatly folded covers. He often awoke chilled with the sweat of the nightmare clammy upon his brow.

On rainy nights, the water falling against the windows of the house further masked whatever noises played in the house. Yet, as if whatever caused those sounds was emboldened by that extra masking noise, the footsteps and the creaks and the snaps became less surreptitious. Billy would gaze toward the door that opened onto the linen corridor leading to the front room. Or he would stare at the lightly curtained windows that looked onto the screened porch. He would strain to hear, and particularly on these rainy nights, he thought he detected voices in the house — whispers, low laughter, and tiny smothered squeals.

Billy grew used to these noises, just as he had grown used to his strictured life. He did not mention them to Elinor or Zaddie. For all he knew, one of them might be sneaking friends into the house; or they might be staying up late together and talking of Oscar and all the others they had seen die. Whoever moved so softly about the house at night wished to remain unknown to Billy. And Billy delicately refused to pry.

One morning just after dawn, one of Billy's worst nightmares returned, and he was so frightened that he woke up rather than allowing it to continue. He

128

immediately forgot its substance, though he knew that whatever it was, he had dreamed it before. He lay still in the bed, feeling the salty sweat drip from his forehead into his eyes. He turned his head and examined the door to the linen closet. He did this every morning, he knew not why, but he was always relieved to find that it had not been opened—though who should open it, or why he thought it might swing open of its own accord, he had no idea. Then he looked in the other direction, and saw the early morning sunlight filtering through the sheer curtains. He could make out the green furniture of the porch dimly, and that too was a comfort. He got out of bed, went into the bathroom, and quietly bathed and shaved; it was fully an hour before his usual time, and he did not wish to disturb Elinor across the hall. He dressed, and then stepped out into the hallway, intending to go downstairs and beg an early cup of coffee from Zaddie. He wondered if he'd have to wake her up.

But Zaddie was not only up, she was kneeling on the staircase landing beneath the great window, wiping up a large puddle of water.

Billy quietly went down the stairs.

"Morning, Zaddie. What happened?" Billy asked.

"I spilled a glass of water," returned Zaddie uneasily.

Billy said nothing, though he didn't believe her. Zaddie didn't like to lie, and lying showed in her face. But even if Zaddie's face had borne the serenity of lying Sapphira's, Billy would have known that it was not a glass of water that spilled there. As he passed Zaddie on his way downstairs, he was assailed with the smell of muddy Perdido water.

He still said nothing, but he noticed that the stairs were *all* damp. Zaddie, then, had just finished mopping up Perdido water from *all* the stairs.

In fact, Billy said nothing about the incident for so long a time that his very silence on the matter seemed to take on substance for him in that sluggish household. Elinor had never said a word about hearing noises or voices at night. Neither had Zaddie. But both Elinor and Zaddie looked at Billy every morning as if they wondered whether *this* morning, he would say anything. And when he never did, the women seemed to look at him in a way that suggested that they approved of his decision to say nothing. This, at least, was Billy's interpretation of what was going on in their minds and was very likely— he thought—only more of his imagination.

Yet as if reassured by his silence, Billy was certain that the noises grew louder, less constrained. Now, beneath the air conditioner, beneath the rain, Billy very definitely made out footsteps; steps that came up the stairs and sometimes went directly into Elinor's room, and sometimes paused at his own door first. Billy would lie in bed, unmoving, but thinking bravely, *Come in. Come in.* But always the steps turned away. Occasionally there was a second set of steps, too, but these were quite different, halting and clumsy, and they never paused at his door. Then would come the voices. He could make out Elinor's voice now—that was easy. The second voice was more difficult to identify. It wasn't Zaddie, of that he was certain. Yet it was familiar. It sounded, in fact, like Frances's voice. But since Frances was dead, it must be someone whose voice made him think of his drowned wife. But he could think of no one, and that bothered him. The third voice wasn't like any that he had ever heard before, sometimes it was a hoarse bleat, and sometimes a kind of singing—singing that was neither happy, sad, reverent, patriotic, or any of the other things he had ever associated with song.

Billy never investigated these phenomena, never attempted to discover their source or identity. They were Elinor's business, he intuited, and he would do nothing that abridged her privacy. Even when he woke earlier than usual, he remained in bed. He would not go out of his room, for he did not want again to surprise Zaddie in the act of mopping up Perdido water from the stairs. He laid no traps, he made no insinuating remarks, he put aside even the appearance of curiosity or puzzlement. This, however, did not mean that his curiosity and puzzlement did not increase, almost daily.

One day in October the air conditioning was turned off, and when Billy went to bed that night he wondered whether the noises would continue as before. They did not, that first night, and he was disappointed. He hardly slept at all, and next morning both Elinor and Zaddie commented on how poorly he looked. "It's because the air conditioner got turned off," he said blandly. "I'm used to all that noise, I guess."

But the following night Billy was pleased to hear the footsteps again, and the two voices: Elinor's and the one that sounded so much like Frances's that he could not imagine its belonging to anyone else. About a week later, the second visitor came as well, and Billy heard quite vividly the clumsy steps upon the stairs, a hoarse muffled bleat in the hallway, and much later in the night, the high-pitched singing. Billy listened and tried to imagine who could be singing thus, a wandering interminable hypnotic song, in accents, and pitches, and rhythms that were wholly unfamiliar.

The autumn passed, winter came on, and Elinor put down carpeting on the stairs. Most mornings it was still damp when Billy came down to breakfast. Elinor always asked him, "How did you sleep last night?"

"Fine," Billy always replied. "I dreamed of Frances. I dreamed Frances came to see us."

One rainy night in February of 1969, Billy lay long awake. Both sets of footsteps had come not long after he had got into bed, and he was upset that the loud patter of the rain kept him from hearing nothing more than an occasional laugh or croaking bleat. Yet that night, just as Billy was finally drifting off to sleep, the singing came again, stronger than ever before; singing that was at once caught in the rhythm of the falling rain, yet running counter to it in such a way that he could catch every quaver of its wandering melody. He listened in delight, and then in wonder when a second voice was united with the first, in precise cadence and then in counterpoint; and his wonder turned to rapture when a third voice joined them. The third voice was Elinor's, and she was singing as neither Billy nor anyone else in Perdido had ever heard her sing. The three voices— *female but not human,* Billy thought—went on for more than an hour, lasting as long as the rain. But as the rain slackened, so did the three voices. When the water was no more than an irregular dripping from the eaves, the singing stopped altogether. Billy had long ago lost the habit of prayer, but now he prayed for the clouds to return, and to open up above the house in hope that the voices might again unite in song. The clouds had flown beyond Perdido, however, and the house was silent except for an occasional drip from the roof. But Billy did not sleep; straining against sleep, he waited for the footsteps to leave Elinor's room. At last, when he thought that dawn must soon be upon them, he was rewarded. The door of Elinor's sitting room softly opened, and he heard the footsteps move out into the hallway. Instead of going directly to the stairs, however, they paused before the door of his room.

This is something else new, Billy thought excitedly.

He had trained his eyes as well as his ears, and he saw quite well in the darkened room. He saw the glass knob of the door turning softly, and it shone a little fractured light into his eyes.

The door was pushed quietly open.

Billy closed his eyes. Whoever it was expected him to be asleep, and he would no more have appeared to be awake than he would have said to Elinor, "Who do you entertain every night in your room?"

Billy's eyes were closed, but he could not refrain from smiling.

See, whispered the voice that was Frances's—but not Frances's, because Frances was dead, drowned in the black waters of the Perdido. *See, Nerita? That's your daddy.*

CHAPTER 82

Mrs. Woskoboinikow

In the spring of 1969, Lilah Bronze graduated from Barnard with high honors. If she hadn't fought relentlessly with her tutor during her senior year she would probably have graduated Summa rather than only Magna cum laude. The Caskeys wondered whether Lilah would return to Perdido, but no one asked her her plans. They would find out quickly enough, and Lilah was just the sort to say, "I have no idea," just for the perversity of it. She returned home once that summer, in August, and then barely long enough to reassure her family that she had taken no part in the campus riots of the previous spring.

"And I'm only here for a week," she said at the Sunday dinner table to which all the Caskeys had gathered to welcome her back. "So nobody run off accepting invitations for me or anything like that."

Elinor and Billy, Miriam and Malcolm all glanced at one another, but for several moments no one said anything. Grace and Lucille said nothing; they did not approve of the manner in which Lilah had always been allowed to go her own way, unchecked. Tommy Lee Burgess simply looked embarrassed. Then, at last, with vast diffidence, Malcolm said, "Ah, Lilah…"

"Yes?" Lilah returned quickly and almost savagely.

Malcolm saw that it was his responsibility to ask the great question, and he cast about in his mind for a framework for it that wouldn't anger Lilah. He at last found a supremely delicate interrogatory: "If you decide to change your telephone number, you might write down the new one and send it to me—just in case there's an emergency or anything."

Lilah nodded, and everyone felt relieved. Lilah was evidently appeased by Malcolm's subtlety.

"In fact," Lilah said, mollified, "I've *already* changed my number. I'll give it to you before I leave."

Billy cleared his throat, and said, "Lilah, did you move out of your old apartment or did you just have the number changed?"

"Why the hell would I change my number unless I moved?" Lilah demanded.

Her father shrugged as if to indicate that nothing Lilah did could astonish him.

"I've moved about two blocks away," Lilah continued reluctantly. It seemed as if her family had ferreted out her most private and long-guarded secret.

"A bigger place?" asked Miriam.

"Yes..." said Lilah thoughtfully. "Yes, it is bigger."

"Higher up?" asked Elinor. "Or lower down?" Previously Lilah had lived on the twenty-first floor.

Lilah didn't answer at once. She glanced around the table, clucked her tongue, sighed, dropped her napkin into her lap, and said, "Well, I guess I may as well go on and tell you..."

"Tell us what?" asked Tommy Lee quickly.

"...because you will worm it out of me before I get out of here, anyway. And if I say it now, maybe you will let me have some peace."

"What is it, honey?" asked Malcolm.

"Two things," said Miriam. "First one is, I'm staying in New York. I'm not coming back here."

"We figured that," said Grace dryly, "when you said you had moved two blocks away."

"And the reason I'm staying is that I'm going to law school in the fall. Columbia again."

The Caskeys all thought about this for a few moments, and then offered their congratulations. It was thought a wise decision; there were so many others she might have made that wouldn't have been wise at all.

"Any particular kind of law?" asked Billy.

"I'm not sure," replied Lilah. "Tax law, probably."

"Good," said Miriam. "Then you'll be able to help us. Billy and I go through I don't know what all every year with those people we hire up in Atlanta."

"Maybe," said Lilah. "Maybe I'll help—and maybe not. Maybe I won't go into tax law at all."

Some discussion followed now on the business of taxes and lawyers in general, a discussion in which Lilah took no part. When finally there was a pause, Lilah spoke up with exasperation, "Well, doesn't anybody want to hear the other part of my news?"

"I thought that was it," said Lucille. "You're staying in New York, and you're going to tax law school."

"That was just one thing," said Lilah peevishly. "I was counting those two as one."

"What else then?" asked Tommy Lee.

Lilah looked around the table to make sure that she had everyone's attention. "Now, I don't want you all to jump all over me," she warned.

No one said anything, and that counted as a promise not to disapprove no matter what she was about to tell them.

"I got married last week," said Lilah. "On Thursday."

The Caskeys said nothing, partly out of shock, and partly in fulfillment of their promise not to express displeasure. She could hardly have said anything more stunning.

Grace, at last, with an exaggerated gesture of peering around the room, said, "Is he here? Did you bring him?"

"I did not," said Lilah definitely.

"You could have," said Miriam. "There's plenty of room."

"He wouldn't come," said Lilah. "I *did* ask him."

"Why not?" asked Billy. "Why wouldn't he come?"

"He hates Alabama," replied Lilah. "He came down here in '64 and '65 for all the civil rights business, and he got hosed down and beaten up and thrown into the Selma jail. He says he will never set foot in Alabama again."

"This man have a name?" asked Lucille.

"His name is Michael."

"Does he have a last name?" asked Miriam.

"Woskoboinikow." The whole table looked blank. Lilah repeated the name very slowly. *"Wosko*—rhymes with *Roscoe. Boin*—like *boing-boing. Ikow*—like *he coughs.* Got it? Woskoboinikow. Real simple. It's Polish. He's not. Or his grandfather was, I guess. He's from Cleveland. So now I'm Lilah Woskoboinikow. I've already had my checks printed up. If you want to see them, I've got them in my bag."

"And what does he do?" asked Billy. "Now that he's out of jail?"

"He's a plasma physicist. A scientist," she explained when everyone regarded her blankly.

The Caskeys shook their heads. It was just like Lilah to have got married without warning to a man with a name that no one had ever heard of or could rightly pronounce or remember how to spell, whose job involved something they had never heard of, and who refused absolutely ever to come to Alabama.

"Are we gone be allowed to meet him?" Miriam asked.

"If you come to New York," said Lilah.

"Let me ask you something," said Miriam.

"What?"

"Does Michael know how much money you have?"

"I don't have any money of my own," Lilah reminded her.

"Does Michael know how much money *we* have then?" Miriam persisted.

"I've told him," Lilah replied. "But I don't think he really realizes it. Michael doesn't know anything about money. I've been handling all his finances for the past year. I don't think he cares."

The Caskeys sighed, and once the immediate shock was over, it occurred to each of them that they should have known all along that it would happen precisely this way.

Tommy Lee Burgess, in his new position as Miriam's assistant in matters relating to the Caskey oil properties, had grown in stature not only in his own eyes but in those of his family and the community at large. He was, in fact, thought quite a catch. He wasn't handsome, and he certainly was overweight, but he was good-natured and kind—and very rich. Tommy Lee, however, showed no interest whatsoever in any one of the thirty or forty thousand marriageable young women in Baldwin County, Alabama, and Escambia County, Florida. Tommy Lee was content to stay at home with Grace and Lucille. His recreation was still hunting and fishing, and occasionally innocently carousing with the men who worked the oil rigs in the swamp south of the farm. The fact was—and all the Caskeys knew it—that Tommy Lee was hopelessly in love with Lilah Bronze; had loved her since the day he had moved in with his grandmother next door to Lilah. He had been mightily disappointed that Lilah did not go to school at Auburn, and now he was more severely distressed to discover that she had up and married a man whose name nobody could even pronounce. He said nothing at the dinner table when Lilah made her startling announcement, but on the drive back to the farm through the dark deserted countryside, he leaned forward from the back seat and, resting his chin on the seat between Grace and Lucille, remarked ruefully, "I could have told everybody. I could have told everybody it was gone happen just this way."

"How would you have known?" asked Lucille. "Nobody could predict that."

"I could have, if I hadn't been foolish. But I wanted to believe that someday Lilah would come back here."

"You're disappointed, aren't you, Tommy Lee?" sighed Grace.

"I sure am," Tommy Lee admitted in the dark.

"You shouldn't be. Look at the way Lilah treats people. I never thought I'd be able to say this about anybody, but Lilah Whatever-her-name-is-now is harder to get along with than Miriam *ever* was. You even wanted to marry her, I guess."

"I would have. I would have married her in a minute."

"And have been miserable from that very minute into all eternity," said Lucille. "She would have led you around by the nose."

"I know it," said Tommy Lee wistfully.

"You know what I think?" said Grace.

"What?"

"I think you ought to go and speak to Lilah and tell her how you feel."

"What good would that do?" said Tommy Lee. "I had my chance. I didn't say anything. Now it's too late."

"Then this is the time to say it," argued Grace. "When it's too late for her to say yes. And you'll get it off your chest. I know you, Tommy Lee. I know you'll carry this around like a two-ton safe on your back unless you go up to Lilah and tell her what you feel."

"Better do it," agreed Tommy Lee's mother.

"Turn the car around," said Tommy Lee, throwing himself mightily against the back seat. "Drive back right now and I'll do it."

But Grace continued on through Babylon toward the farm. "Go tomorrow," she advised. "Do it in the daylight."

So Tommy Lee drove back to Perdido the following morning and arrived before Lilah was even up. Melva had delivered Lilah's breakfast on a tray, and Lilah was sitting up in bed. Tommy Lee knocked on the

139

door jamb, and Lilah said, as she buttered her toast, "Miriam's already gone down to the mill, Tommy Lee. I don't know where the hell Malcolm's gone off to."

"I came to see you," said Tommy Lee.

"Then come on in and sit on the edge of the bed," said Lilah. She looked up and smiled at him. Lilah was a handsome girl, the handsomest girl Tommy Lee had ever known, and once Tommy Lee had gone out with the Auburn homecoming queen. Lilah's smile was radiant, and it was also the kindest greeting she had ever given him.

"What are you doing here?" Tommy Lee began awkwardly.

"I am eating my breakfast. You know, you can't get grits in New York for love nor money."

"No, I mean, what are you doing in Perdido? If you just got married last week, why aren't you on your honeymoon?"

"Michael couldn't get off right away. We're going down to the Caribbean in the winter sometime. It doesn't matter anyway. I hate all that business."

"What business?" asked Tommy Lee.

"Wedding business," returned Lilah. "That's why I didn't tell anybody. I didn't want anybody to do anything. We went down to city hall. It was very impersonal," she added with something very like pride.

Tommy Lee shifted his weight on the bed, nearly upsetting Lilah's tray.

"You are big as a house, Tommy Lee," Lilah remarked. "If you don't be still, I'm going to make you move over to a chair."

"I've missed you all that time you've been in New York," said Tommy Lee.

"And I've missed you, too," said Lilah, blowing on her coffee to cool it.

"Have you?"

"Yes. I wouldn't say so if I hadn't. I didn't miss

140

Grace and Lucille, for instance. I did miss you, though."

Tommy Lee was silent for a few moments, not knowing how to go on. Melva came up again to see if everything was all right with the breakfast, and Lilah asked her to bring a tray for Tommy Lee.

"I just ate out at the farm," Tommy Lee protested.

"You haven't stopped at just one breakfast in ten years," said Lilah. "Have another one, and keep me company."

"So you're going to be a lawyer," said Tommy Lee, putting off the inevitable.

"I intend to make a *fortune*," said Lilah vehemently.

"Why?"

"What do you mean, 'Why?' Everybody wants to make a lot of money."

"You *have* a lot of money, Lilah."

"I don't have one thing that's mine," said Lilah.

"If you wanted it, all you'd have to do is ask somebody for it. Just ask the first person in the family you ran up against and they'd write you a check for a million dollars, I know they would."

"I know they would, too," said Lilah quietly. "And you know me, Tommy Lee. You'd know I'd never ask."

Tommy Lee shrugged. "I guess," he said. Melva brought another breakfast on a tray and Tommy Lee moved to a wide chair. When Melva had left, Tommy Lee said, "Lilah, you want me to write you a big check? I would, you know, and I'd be pleased to do it. I'd keep it a secret, too. Nobody'd find out about it."

Lilah looked up and considered this. "Tommy Lee," she said, "would it make you happy if I let you pay for my law school?"

"It sure would!"

"Then I'll let you do it. Don't tell anybody, though."

"I won't," Tommy Lee promised. "But you know, they're gone figure it out."

141

"I know that," said Lilah. "Just don't *you* be the one to tell them."

For a few minutes they ate in silence, and then Tommy Lee said, "You know what?"

"What?"

"I have been hoping and hoping that you would come back to Perdido."

"I'm here."

"I mean for good," said Tommy Lee. "'Cause you know why?"

"Why?"

"'Cause when you got back, I was gone ask you to marry me."

"I know that," said Lilah.

"You did!"

"Of course I knew that, Tommy Lee. Every fool in town knew that. And I'm no fool."

"So you would have said no?"

Lilah considered this. "Maybe. Maybe not." She considered a few moments more. "Probably I would have said no."

"Why?" Tommy Lee asked with more curiosity than chagrin.

"Because that's what everybody would have wanted. That's what everybody would have expected. If I had married you, it would have been just like Miriam and Malcolm all over again. I didn't want that. It's not that I think you and I would have been unhappy, Tommy Lee, it's just that I have no intention of hanging around this place doing what people expect me to do."

"So you married that other man instead?"

"That's right."

"Is he as smart as you are, Lilah?"

"No. He's not even as smart as you are, Tommy Lee, not when it comes to practical stuff. But Michael knows a lot about plasma physics, and I guess he'll probably be important someday. And he does what I tell him to."

"Guess he'd have to do that."

142

They were silent for a few minutes, then Lilah sent Tommy Lee down to the kitchen for more coffee. When he came back up, she had put aside the tray and brushed the crumbs off the covers onto the floor. She sat up straight in the bed, brushing her hair.

"Don't you be upset now," she warned him.

"About what?" he asked, pouring coffee into the cup that she had placed on the bedside table.

"About me not marrying you."

"I'm not upset," said Tommy Lee. "I told you, I'm just disappointed. I'm real unhappy, but I'm not upset."

"Now I'm going to tell you something," said Lilah. "But I'm not going to tell you this unless you promise not to breathe a word of it to anybody—not Grace and Lucille, not Miriam, not Elinor, and not anybody."

"I promise," said Tommy Lee solemnly. "You want me to shut the door?"

"Nobody's around," said Lilah, dismissing that suggestion. "I want you to do something for me."

"Anything."

"I want you to be smart."

"Lilah, I'm not sure—"

"I want you to learn everything there is to learn about those damned wells out there, and whatever else it is that makes this family so damned much money."

"That I can do."

"And then you come up to New York and you visit Michael and me and tell me all about it. Everything you can find out, you understand?"

"All right," said Tommy Lee.

Lilah smiled. Indulgently, she condescended to explain: "I'm going to inherit from somebody somewhere along the line. Maybe from Daddy, maybe from Miriam, maybe from Elinor—who knows? So then I'm going to be rich. I'm also going to be a lawyer. Now what nobody else knows here is that at Columbia I majored in business."

143

"Business!"

"Shhh! Yes. I told everybody I was majoring in English, but really and truly I majored in business." Her brush was caught in a tangle of her long hair and she paused until she had drawn it free. "And what I intend to do is come back here sometime—*sometime*, Tommy Lee, so don't be getting your hopes up—and you and I are going to show this place what we can do. We're going to have more money than we know what to do with."

"We have that already," Tommy Lee pointed out.

"Then we're going to have five times that. And you and I are going to do it together."

"Are you thinking of a divorce?" he asked innocently. "Already?"

Lilah pointed her brush at him menacingly. "You are beginning to ask too many questions, Tommy Lee Burgess."

CHAPTER 83

Champagne Toasts

Elinor announced that she wanted to give a little party for Lilah before she went back to New York to celebrate her marriage to the unknown Dr. Michael Woskoboinikow. Lilah reluctantly agreed, but only because Lilah had affection and respect for her grandmother. "I just don't want too many people," Lilah remarked. "I don't want to get my arm shaken off and have to answer five hundred stupid questions about New York City. That's what I don't want."

"It will be just family," returned Elinor. "Since Michael isn't here, we can't very well ask anybody *but* family. There would be too many questions."

"You mean just have everybody for dinner one night, that's all you mean?" Lilah asked, relieved.

"Yes," replied Elinor. "But just a bit more formal than usual. If you didn't bring any, get Miriam to lend you some of her jewelry."

So Elinor Caskey planned a small family dinner party for the night before Lilah was to fly back to New York. Billy and Malcolm and Tommy Lee bought new black dinner jackets, and Grace and Lucille went to Pensacola and bought new gowns. The dining room table was to be set with Mary-Love's wedding china, Elinor's best cut-glass crystal, and a set of James's silver that had been taken out of the house before it burned.

No one knew why, but there was something melancholy about the preparations for this occasion. Perhaps it was the unwonted care that Elinor took with it, fussing over details in a fashion that wasn't

145

common with her. She sent Malcolm to New Orleans for a new tablecloth, and arranged for a florist to come up from Mobile to arrange the flowers on Friday morning. Zaddie and Luvadia and Melva were to serve, and each of these three black women got new gray uniforms just for that evening.

"Elinor," Billy asked curiously, seeing all this business afoot, "are you planning on something special?"

"No," Elinor replied after a few moments. "This is all just because we weren't able to give Lilah a proper wedding..."

Friday night came, and all that remained of the family gathered at Elinor's. Malcolm arrived first and set up equipment needed to mix drinks, all such tasks long having fallen to his lot. Then Billy came downstairs to keep Malcolm company, and soon Lucille, Grace, and Tommy Lee arrived in their rarely driven Cadillac. Lucille, distressed by a new girdle, and Grace, a little unsure of her high heels, came up the front steps just as Elinor was coming down the stairs from the second floor. Miriam and Lilah came last, a strange pair making their way across the sandy yards in the refulgent Southern twilight; Miriam in purple velvet and diamonds and Lilah in green silk and emeralds.

They mounted the front steps and went onto the porch. Miriam knocked softly on the screen door. Zaddie appeared in her new starched uniform and opened the door.

"Evening, Miss Miriam. Evening, Miss Lilah."

"Evening, Zaddie," returned Miriam. "Everybody here?"

"Everybody here but you. And y'all sure are pretty tonight."

"Thank you," said Lilah simply, and actually blushed for the compliment.

Zaddie opened the doors of the front parlor, and Miriam marched directly in, saying, "Malcolm, have you fixed me a drink yet?"

Lilah lingered a little behind Zaddie, and then, as if gathering her courage—or maybe realizing that courage should not be an issue when only in the midst of her own family—Lilah entered the room, and sat next to Tommy Lee on the couch.

Zaddie and Luvadia then brought in two coolers with bottles of champagne. Malcolm opened the bottles and poured.

At Elinor's direction, Zaddie and Luvadia returned with Melva, and the three women stood in the doorway. They were given glasses of the champagne as well.

"The first toast," said Elinor, standing with her back to the front window, just in the place where Miriam remembered finding Mary-Love in her coffin, "is to Lilah, who is, at least for the time being, the last of the Caskeys. The next toasts will be to the Caskeys who have died. This party is as much in remembrance of them as it is in celebration of Lilah's marriage. Lilah, I hope you don't mind..."

Lilah shook her head and smiled. "No, ma'am," she said softly. "Not a bit."

The room was lighted softly, by candles and by sconces only. Was it that flattering illumination that made Lilah seem so suddenly altered, so softened?

Elinor smiled and continued. "I want to toast Oscar," said Elinor quite simply. "I don't know if any of you—except for Billy and Zaddie—have realized how much I miss him, and how empty this house seems to be without him. Whenever I hear his radio upstairs, I have to stop myself from hoping that it is Oscar, sitting in his chair and turning the dial from one ball game to the other. I think to myself, 'That's Billy, that's not Oscar.' Mary-Love used to say that the reason I came to this town was in order to snare her son. She always said that I was lying in wait for him—and for nobody else—upstairs in the Osceola in the flood of 1919." Elinor smiled. "Mary-Love was right. And this toast is for Oscar."

She raised her glass. They all raised their glasses,

147

and drank off the champagne. Malcolm went quietly around, pouring more.

"This next is for Sister," Elinor went on, "whom we all loved, and whom Miriam loved most of all. Poor Sister! She was never allowed to do anything on her own, never allowed to have anything or feel anything that was hers alone. She loved or hated always in contrariness. She fought all of her life, and I don't think any of us ever really knew how hard those battles were for her. Sister, more than anybody I think, got to the root of this family, because of all of us, she was the most desperate. She fought harder and she clung harder, and when she changed—in the end—she changed more than any of us could ever have imagined possible. She became Mary-Love all over again, the one she hated most, the one that she loved the most. She was unhappy all her life, desperately unhappy, and if she came back now, if she walked in those doors and had a chance to do it all over again, I know she'd say, 'I want everything just the same.' So here's to Sister, whom I miss very, very much."

She raised her glass. They all raised their glasses, and again drank off the champagne.

Elinor went on: "One more. Just one more. For James and Queenie and Mary-Love. All of you remember them as parents, and aunts and uncles, but I don't. I remember them differently. For one thing, I was the only one who was able to fight with Mary-Love on an even basis. And I was the only one who ever *won* a fight with her. I'm not going to say I miss her. Miriam, I wouldn't lie to you even about that. Her coffin stood right here, right where I'm standing. She died in the room directly above this one. I wasn't one bit sorry at the time, and I'm not one bit sorry now. I know how unhappy she made Oscar, I know what she did to Sister. And, Miriam—you're not going to appreciate my saying this—I know what she did to you." Miriam sat stiffly, staring at Elinor, but not venturing to object. "I wonder sometimes if

148

I made a mistake in giving you up to Mary-Love. Mary-Love and I fought and we fought hard—harder than most of you can imagine, even now—and Miriam, you got caught in the middle."

Elinor paused, as if she expected Miriam to speak.

Miriam did so, but with obvious reluctance. "I've never really forgiven you, Mama, that's true. I know we get along all right these days, but you're so old—and I'm getting up there myself. I've got Mary-Love's ring now, the one you stole off her when she was dead. And I managed to get Lilah away from you, and that made me feel better. But I don't think I ever really forgave you, and I don't think that I ever will."

"I know that," said Elinor. "But the question is, if it could all be done over again right from the beginning, would you change anything?"

"No," replied Miriam, without hesitation. "Not a bit."

"Just like Sister," murmured Grace. "Poor Sister."

"And poor James," said Elinor, "and poor Queenie. Mary-Love walked all over James because James let her. Mary-Love couldn't stand Queenie because Queenie was a Strickland, but she didn't have Genevieve's class. I remember when Queenie came to town. Malcolm, you were a little boy—a mean little boy. And Lucille, you were a whiner. I never saw a child who cried more than you did. And all Queenie could think about was getting herself taken care of by James. But Queenie changed—and it was James's doing—because James took her seriously, and I don't think anybody had ever taken Queenie seriously before. Lucille, I hope you miss her."

"I do!" cried Lucille. "I sure do!"

"I do, too," said Malcolm.

"And me, too," said Tommy Lee.

"And I miss Daddy," sighed Grace.

"Y'all," cried Lucille, grasping Grace's hand and wringing it tightly, "all this is making me so sad. Let's don't talk about it anymore. Let's don't talk

149

about all the people who have died. I thought this was a party for Lilah, and Lilah's getting married to what's-his-name."

"Woskoboinikow," said Lilah. "His name is Woskoboinikow. And so is mine now. But you know what, Lucille?"

"What?" said Lucille.

"We all die," said Lilah. "All of us. Every one of us in this room is going to die, sooner or later. Every one of us."

"But we don't have to talk about it!" cried Lucille.

"Y'all," said Zaddie from the doorway. "It's about time y'all sat down to the table. All my good food's gone get cold if you don't."

The Caskeys drank the last of the champagne in their glasses, put the glasses aside, and filed into the dining room.

Lilah, as guest of honor, was seated at the foot of the table in Oscar's old place, and Elinor had her accustomed place at the head.

In lieu of a blessing, Elinor said, "Here we are, the Caskeys who remain. We are fewer than we used to be, and we are—I am happy to say—much richer than we used to be. We have, in fact, everything that I always hoped that we would have. Yet things never turn out quite the way you think they will. But that doesn't matter, not in the least. Sister and Miriam are right. No matter what you've gone through, no matter what you've done and suffered, no matter what horrible mistakes you've made, no matter what you've given up that you should have held on to, no matter what you've held on to that you should have let go, no matter what has happened to make you unhappy, you cannot wish for it to have happened any other way." She looked around the table. Zaddie came in with the first of the dishes, a platter of pheasant that Tommy Lee had shot and hung the month before. Elinor smiled and fingered the ropes of black pearls about her neck. "Thank you, Zaddie," she said.

"Zaddie's gone to a great deal of trouble for us to-night."

"No trouble..." murmured Zaddie perfunctorily, but her denial was made with pride.

"Look at us, Zaddie," said Elinor.

"Ma'am?"

"Look at us, Zaddie, because it's the last time you'll ever see us all together like this. Lilah is right: we all die. And there is somebody standing out there in the graveyard tonight, leaning on Mary-Love's tombstone, and he's flipping a coin to see which one of us is next."

The dinner was substantial, and it seemed that there was no end to the dishes that Zaddie, Luvadia, and Melva brought out of the kitchen. Malcolm had not anticipated more than three bottles of wine being drunk, but as things turned out he had to open a fourth bottle, and then a fifth. Afterward, when the dishes had been cleared and two pots of coffee put out—one for Miriam, and one for everyone else— Malcolm and Billy lighted cigars. In the last stage of this evening, the conversation was mostly between Miriam and Lilah, and it turned again to the Cas- keys' peculiar habit of stealing away one another's children.

Miriam didn't go into that subject directly, but her tack was nevertheless controversial. She said bluntly, "I hope you're gone be happy with that man, Lilah."

"I intend to be," said Lilah, equally as bluntly.

"The fact is," said Miriam, and this was her point, "we were all hoping a little that you and *Tommy Lee* would get married."

Lilah and Tommy Lee exchanged glances.

"Lilah wasn't in love with me," said Tommy Lee. "Too bad."

"That's a matter of opinion," remarked Grace, not entirely beneath her breath.

"I suppose it would have been more convenient

151

for everybody if I had married Tommy Lee," said Lilah. "Convenient for everybody but me, I mean."

"You and Tommy Lee could have taken over around here when I am old and gray," said Miriam.

"We could have taken over when you were dead, Miriam," retorted Lilah. "I don't see you giving up too much of your power *until* then."

"Maybe not," agreed Miriam. The other Caskeys sat back farther in their chairs, leaving room for the two bejeweled women. "Maybe not," Miriam repeated, "but I've been good to Tommy Lee, haven't I? I've given him things to do."

"You've been real good to me," said Tommy Lee to Miriam. "She's taught me a lot," he said to the assemblage in general. "She's given me a lot of responsibility."

"There was another reason I would have liked for Lilah to marry Tommy Lee," Miriam went on, rushing in over the end of Tommy's grateful speech.

"What else?" asked Lucille curiously.

"Malcolm and I have been lonely next door all by ourselves. I was hoping that Lilah and Tommy Lee would have a baby. That's all." Miriam poured another cup of coffee. "Zaddie," she said to the black woman who was passing through the room just then, "would you bring me a bigger cup, please? I'm gone be pouring out of this pot all night long if you don't."

"You'd want me to have a baby so you could steal it," said Lilah. "Just like you stole me."

"Yes," Miriam admitted calmly. "Except I would have gotten this one real young. I was really hoping for it, Lilah. Malcolm and I really have been pretty lonesome since you went off."

Billy said: "Now you know how Elinor and I felt when you took Lilah away from *us*." It was not an accusatory remark, it was only an observation.

Miriam didn't reply to this, but to Lilah she said: "You think you and this boy might think about having a baby?"

"He wants one," said Lilah. "I don't."

"Why not?" asked Lucille.

"Because I see no point in going through months of discomfort and pain so that Miriam can get on a plane and come up to New York and take it away from me."

"I don't think it's *that* much pain," said Miriam. "Besides, I'd sent Melva or somebody up there to take care of you, if that's what you're worried about. I don't even care if it's a boy or a girl, and neither does Malcolm. And you can pick out any name you want. You can call it Shadrach-Meshach-and-Abednego if you want to."

"No," said Lilah bluntly. "I won't do it."

"Miriam," said Grace in indignant astonishment, "you are just like Mary-Love. You can't pour a cup of coffee without its being a plot."

Zaddie had brought the larger cup, and Miriam filled it with coffee.

"I'm not plotting," she said. "I just thought it would be nice to have a baby. Malcolm and I got married too late. And everybody in this room has had the pleasure of raising a child except for Malcolm and me."

"Then go out and find one," suggested Lilah sharply. "Visit an orphanage. Put an ad in the paper."

"I want a *Caskey* baby," said Miriam. "It has to be a *Caskey* baby."

Lilah said nothing.

Quite calmly, Miriam continued: "After all I've done for you, after all that I've given you, you wouldn't say 'thank you' if you were tied to the stake and I was holding a lighted match."

"Thank you, Miriam," Lilah said, "for everything you've done for me. But I still won't give you a little baby."

CHAPTER 84

The Nest

"I'm sorry," said Billy, when everyone had gone home and he and Elinor were ascending to their bedrooms, "that Miriam and Lilah had to have words like that."

"Miriam was just being Miriam," said Elinor, shaking her head with a smile, "and Lilah was being Lilah. I don't imagine there was any harm done. They walked home together, didn't they? And next week Miriam will fly up to New York and meet that man Lilah married."

"What do you think?" said Billy, pausing on the staircase landing. He had with him the last half bottle of champagne and a glass.

"About what?" asked Elinor, leaning for a moment against the frame of the great staircase window. They could hear Zaddie and Melva down in the dining room, clattering silverware and crystal as they cleared the room.

"About that baby business? Do you think that if Lilah had a baby, Miriam would try to steal it?"

"Yes," said Elinor. "I think she probably would."

"Do you think that's right?" Billy poured himself a glass of the champagne. "Should I have brought up another glass?" he asked parenthetically.

Elinor shook her head. "I don't know if it's right or not," she said. "Besides, what right do I have to say anything about it? I'm the one who started the whole business by giving up Miriam. The question should be: was *that* right?"

"Was it?"

Elinor started up the short flight of stairs from

the landing to the second floor. "Why are you drinking that champagne?" she asked. "Didn't you have enough wine with dinner?"

"I hate to see it go to waste," said Billy, "and thinking of Frances made me sad." He followed Elinor up; she stood in the door of her sitting room.

"Frances?" she repeated.

"When you were toasting everyone who was dead," Billy said, "why did you leave out Frances?"

"Billy," said Elinor, "drink your champagne and go to bed. It's been a long evening."

Billy turned away and went into his own room. He crossed over to the window that looked out at Miriam's house. He could see Miriam and Lilah putting away the jewels they had worn. He stood there sipping his champagne, until all the lights were extinguished in Miriam's house and his bottle was empty. Then he took off his clothes and got into bed. Without thought or reflection of any sort, he fell asleep.

He awoke sometime later; how much later he had no way of knowing. But it *seemed* late. His head ached, and he lay very still, pressing his fingers against his brow, hoping to suppress some of the throbbing. That did nothing. He went into the bathroom, swallowed two aspirin, and wiped his face with a damp cloth. That helped. He returned to his bedroom, and then, with the throbbing not so strong in his brain, he heard the voices. As usual, they came from Elinor's room. The champagne had made him forget about them when he lay down upon the bed, and the champagne now made him abandon his studied timidity in the matter of Elinor's visitors. Without any reflection on the consequences of his action, he went to the door to the hallway and opened it softly. The voices were louder now, but because Elinor's sitting room door was closed, he still could not make out what was being said.

He recognized, as before, the voice that was his

wife's—except that Frances was dead, drowned in the black water of the Perdido.

Billy stepped out into the hallway. The carpet was damp beneath his feet. He could smell the water, and knew that it was from the river. It felt gritty on the soles of his feet, and he knew that to be Perdido mud. He walked across to the door of Elinor's sitting room. He quietly turned the knob and inched the door open.

He wasn't so startled by the sudden clarity of Elinor's voice as he was by the light from her bedroom that fell suddenly aslant the leg of his pajamas. He stood still and listened.

"...too late," Elinor said.

"No, it's not," came the other voice, Frances's, except that Frances was drowned. "No, it's not, Mama. But it's going to be if you stay here. You're old, you're so old. And it hurts me when I see you getting older every day. I come to see you whenever I can, whenever I can make the change—but that's not all the time. And Nerita *never* makes it—I don't think she can. What happens if I can't do it anymore? You should come stay with us, Mama. If you came back with us, you wouldn't get old, you might even get young again. Mama, Nerita and I would take good care of you!"

"I don't want to leave, darling."

"Why not? What's keeping you here? Daddy's dead. James is dead. Queenie is dead."

"Billy—" said Elinor.

"Billy stays here because of you. He doesn't want to leave you alone, that's all. If you went away, Billy would go off somewhere and have him a good time, I know he would, and it'd be good for him, too. Poor old Billy! You know, the other night I opened the door of my old room, and there was Billy—"

"You shouldn't have! What if you had waked him up?"

"Mama," laughed the someone who couldn't have been Frances, though she had Frances's voice and

156

called Elinor Mama, "don't you think Billy knows something's going on?"

"He's never said anything."

"Neither has Zaddie. Don't you think Zaddie knows?"

"Zaddie *certainly* knows," agreed Elinor.

"And Billy does, too. Anyway, he didn't wake up. And I wanted to show Nerita what her daddy looked like."

"What did Nerita think?" Elinor asked curiously.

"She thought he looked old. And he does. Poor old Billy."

Billy pushed open the sitting room door all the way and then stepped into the light. Elinor sat in one of the plush new armchairs she had bought after Oscar's death, and on the edge of the bed sat Frances, his wife. Yet it wasn't Frances. It couldn't have been, for Frances had been born in 1922, and would have been nearly fifty now, had she not drowned in the Perdido. This Frances was no more than thirty-two or thirty-three, and she looked like the Frances that Billy last remembered.

"Frances?" said Billy.

Frances laughed, drawing her cotton robe across her breast. "Hey, Billy," she said shyly. "Why haven't you gotten married in all these years?"

"Billy," said Elinor, not sternly but sadly, "go back to bed."

Billy stepped further into the room. He stood behind Elinor's chair, and looked at his wife.

"Are you alive?" he asked.

"No," said Elinor.

Frances shook her head. "No," she said. "I'm not."

"Who is Nerita?" Billy asked.

"Nerita is your other little girl," said Frances. "Nerita didn't come tonight."

"But some nights she does come," said Billy. "And she sings?"

"You've heard her?" asked Elinor, looking up at Billy over her shoulder.

157

"Yes," said Billy, "I've heard her. And when you opened my door the other night, I *was* awake, but I didn't open my eyes."

"Go back to bed," said Elinor.

"You're not sad about me, are you?" Frances asked curiously.

Billy shook his head. "I never was," he admitted.

"Good," said Frances. "Then go back to bed, Billy, and whenever you hear Nerita and me coming upstairs to visit Mama, don't come out, understand?"

"You're dead," he said quietly. "You don't look dead. You live at the bottom of the junction, don't you? I remember, on the day we decided to get married, you took me on top of the levee and we went down and looked at the junction, and you told me that you had been down there. And that's where you are now, isn't it—at the bottom of the junction."

"Billy—" Elinor began.

"Are you going back with Frances?" Billy asked his mother-in-law.

"Yes, she is," answered Frances quickly.

"No, I'm not," said Elinor. "I'm going to stay here with you, Billy."

"Mama—"

"Shhh!" said Elinor. "I made my choice a long time ago, Frances. I made my choice on Easter Sunday of 1919, when I sat on the edge of that bed in the corner room of the Osceola. I'm not going back on that choice now."

"You could come back, Mama!"

Elinor shook her head. She seemed to have forgotten that Billy was there, or perhaps she wanted him to hear.

"I can't go back," she said. "You make the choice once, and that's all. You were born here, in this room, darling, and you made the choice to go back to the river. I was born—well, I wasn't born in any feather bed—and one day when this whole town was under water, I saw a white man and a colored man rowing

158

along in a little green boat and I made *my* decision. So I'll finish out my time here."

"Mama, it's such a waste!" cried Frances.

"It's not a waste. I haven't regretted it for one single minute. Not even when Oscar died and I knew that it was Mary-Love and John Robert DeBordenave who killed him—that he died because of me and what I had done to them. I didn't even regret that, darling."

Frances slipped down off the edge of the bed onto the floor at her mother's feet.

"Mama, what will Nerita and I do without you? How am I supposed to let you grow old and die? You're already *so* old now!"

"There's nothing you can do, darling. Not a thing. I have Billy here"—she hadn't forgotten him, and reached up and grasped his hand—"and Billy will take care of me. Billy, that's why I've kept you on."

"Why?" he asked.

"To take care of me when I die."

"Elinor—" he began to protest.

"You and Zaddie are going to have to protect me," she said in a quiet voice.

"Protect you from what?" Frances cried, looking up into her mother's face.

"When the time comes, they'll know."

"Nerita and I will protect you! We'll protect you from whatever it is."

"You won't be able to," said Elinor, "but Billy and Zaddie will be here."

"Mama, do you know when it's going to be?"

Elinor only smiled. "I promise you, darling, that before it happens, I will come out into the river once more—just once more—and say goodbye to you and Nerita."

The day after the melancholy party, Lilah went back to New York and Mr. Woskoboinikow. Tommy Lee, distressed and forlorn, threw himself into the Caskey oil business with redoubled ardor. He was down at the wells every morning in time to speak to the third-shift workers before they drove back to their trailer homes in Cantonement and Jay. He talked to Miriam and to Billy on the telephone two or three times each day, and more than once he went with Miriam on business trips and was introduced about by her. Elinor helped him in the selection of several new suits for these trips, and on the whole Tommy Lee made a good impression—if nothing else, he looked *substantial*. Besides, he came with Miriam's recommendation, and that counted for a lot in New York, Houston, and New Orleans.

It gradually became known in Babylon and Perdido that Tommy Lee had been disappointed in love. He had hoped, and all his family had hoped, that he would marry Lilah Bronze; but Lilah, herself trained by Miriam, had done a sort of Miriam-like thing and married herself to a man with a name that was two inches long and who declared on a stack of Bibles that he would never set foot in Alabama again. The civil rights business in Selma hadn't been all that long ago, and people hadn't quite forgiven the Northerners, the new Carpetbaggers, who had come down and interfered so mischievously. And Lilah Bronze had gone off and *married* one of those unprincipled men. However, through all this Tommy Lee had gained some depth in the eyes of the community because of his broken heart; people understood that he threw himself into his work in order to forget. Mamas kept their daughters away, "until the boy finds himself again." Tommy Lee, by this crook of history, became an adult without the burden of actually having to get married, the usual rite of passage in a man's development in Alabama.

Lucille and Grace were proud of Tommy Lee. They never forgot to thank God in their prayers each night, as they knelt beside each other at the edge of the bed, that Tommy Lee hadn't rebelled and run off to Chicago to fight the police, that he hadn't grown his hair long or swallowed LSD. They gave thanks that he was there with them most days at lunchtime, and every evening at suppertime; and that his laughter, raucous and echoing, could be heard all over the house at night as he watched television with his friends from the oil rigs.

Late one morning in the spring of 1970, Tommy Lee was paddling his boat through the swamp in a course that was as directly northward as the waterways and hummocks would allow. He didn't like to use the motor because of the noise it made and the smell of gasoline that poured up out of it, and besides, the exercise always served to increase his appetite, and considering the tortuousness of the swamp, paddling wasn't that much slower. He had spent the morning with the oilmen at rigs number 5 and 8, and was now heading back to the farm for lunch. He had grown used to the swamp, and knew his way about well enough to find his way in and out, which was all that really mattered. He kept a small boat tethered at the southern extremity of the farm proper, just where the swamp began. In the bottom of the boat and under a tight tarpaulin, he had stored a case of beer, the rifle that Elinor had given him for Christmas a few years back, and the latest men's magazines in a plastic bag. The men's magazines were for himself—he was fearful of Grace or Lucille coming across them in the house; the beer was for the oil rig workers; and the rifle was for the alligators who occasionally swam lazily after his small boat, as if in hope that so large a morsel as Tommy Lee Burgess would faint from the heat and tumble over the edge of the boat into the oily water.

This morning, with his stomach growling, Tommy Lee paddled alone through the swamp, thinking of nothing but the lunch he knew that Luvadia was preparing for him. He had reached a point about a mile from the northernmost oil rig, but still half a mile from where he kept the boat tied up. By the sun's position he knew he was heading in the right

161

direction, so he didn't pay much attention to the particular scenery through which he was passing. It all looked very much alike in one place as another anyway.

Tommy Lee decided that Luvadia was cooking either fried corn or okra for him. The more he thought about it he hoped that it wasn't going to be just okra, and no fried corn at all. Tommy Lee didn't understand how *anyone* could like okra unless it was deepfried with lots of batter, and then you had to pretend it was soggy shrimp inside. His boat must have passed over a shallow spot, for his paddle suddenly caught in the mud. The boat jerked, and Tommy Lee fell forward, knocking his knees painfully against the case of beer.

He had let go of the paddle, and it remained sticking upward in that mud. The boat wavered and swayed as Tommy Lee righted himself and reached for the paddle.

The paddle suddenly lifted itself and flew high into the air.

Tommy Lee, astounded, watched its ascent, and his mouth fell open as it hung in the air for a moment before falling back into the water, twenty yards or so from the boat.

Tommy Lee looked over the side, and saw that something looked back at him through the oily black water—a round flat face, either green or black, he couldn't tell for certain, with perfectly circular bulging eyes, a wide lipless mouth, and two dilated holes for nostrils.

It was not his reflection, for it distinctly lay beneath the surface of the water. It was not at all like an alligator, or any kind of fish ever caught in these— or any other—waters. It was not a drowned animal snared in the submerged roots of one of the cypresses. It was not anything at all within Tommy Lee's experience. And Tommy Lee didn't have a paddle anymore.

He turned right around in the boat, and pulled

the cord on the motor, praying that it would start. *Last week*, he thought, *that's when I used it last. No, not last week, last month*.

The motor didn't start.

Tommy Lee pulled the cord again. The motor gurgled, then died.

Suddenly the boat was jerked backward. Tommy Lee lost his balance for a moment and slipped awkwardly off the seat onto the bottom of the boat. As he struggled to get back up, at the same time reaching for the motor, the boat was tipped precariously to the right. Tommy Lee reached out to grab the sides of the boat in an attempt to right it by casting his weight to the left, but his right hand touched not the edge of the boat, but something else—something quite wet and slippery.

He jerked his hand away and looked. There was an arm, definitely greenish-gray and not black at all, ending in a wide, splayed, webbed hand, thrust over the edge of the boat. The hand was pressed flat against the seat.

Tommy Lee grabbed the plastic package of men's magazines and hit the hand with it. The hand didn't even flinch. Tommy Lee flung the magazines aside, picked up the rifle and banged the hand with the butt. The hand seemed to curl slightly and give a little quiver, but it remained pressed against the seat. Tommy Lee realized then that the boat was moving slowly away to the right. The thing wasn't trying to climb up into the boat, it was only swimming away with it.

Tommy Lee didn't dare look over the side.

He turned the rifle around and took aim at the hand. Yet he did not shoot, suddenly realizing that the bullet might pierce not only the hand, but the seat and the bottom of the boat as well. He did not relish foundering in the swamp with *that*.

He tried, without making too much disturbance, to get the motor going but it would not start. The boat was moving inexorably toward one of the larger hummocks in that part of the swamp, one that Tommy Lee recognized; one to which he had even given a name. He called it the Nest, because of all the alligators' nests that fringed it.

Not knowing what else to do, he sat next to the motor and repeatedly pulled the cord, keeping an eye on the hand as he did so and trying to keep the rifle from slipping off his lap.

The motor started at last. He turned the rudder, and gave it all the gas.

The boat still moved inexorably toward the Nest. The power of the motor could not affect the direction of the boat by even a single degree.

With his leg pressed against the rudder to keep it in position, Tommy Lee raised the rifle and stared through the sights at the elbow of the creature where it appeared atop the edge of the boat. When it stood out of the water—if it could stand—Tommy Lee would shoot it.

He now began to think that the boat was moving too slowly. *Faster, faster,* he thought. Every few seconds, he had to wipe away the sweat on his hands and brow.

As the boat neared the Nest, for once he saw no alligators. All the nests appeared to have been abandoned. He heard no birds, but he did hear something else. A singing—there was no other word for it—high-pitched, droning, like nothing he had ever heard. He peered into the high grass and the trunks of the cypress on the Nest but could see nothing. Then, at the same moment that he noticed two mounds of dried grass that looked almost like huts large enough for a large man to crawl into half-hidden among the dense scrub, he heard a second voice in unison with the first. After a few moments, however, it branched off into a melody of its own, with a slightly different quality. The boat was being drawn ever nearer the large hummock of dry grass, massive cypress, and tangled underbrush.

Then, quite without warning, the boat swung

around and floated alongside the hummock, past half a dozen large empty alligator nests. In some of them Tommy Lee could count the eggs, and when did alligators ever abandon their eggs? He could hear the two voices quite clearly now. Through the sight of the rifle he picked out their locations on the hummock. He was quite certain of their positions in that high grass; he wondered if he ought to shoot. Without even having consciously made that decision, he cocked the rifle and was about to pull the trigger when he was startled by the sound of something pulling up out of the water, and the addition of a third voice to that singing, a third voice that at first was gurgly, but soon became as clear and pristine as the two others. Over the edge of the boat, Tommy Lee saw a large flat perfectly smooth head. Its features were turned away from him.

Tommy Lee moved the gun forward until the barrel was no more than a foot from the back of that glistening head.

"Nerita!" The word came sharply across the water from the high grass.

The head disappeared beneath the water.

Tommy Lee automatically swung the rifle and took aim for the place from where he had heard the voice. He pulled the trigger and the rifle fired, knocking him painfully against the motor with its recoil. The boat had evidently been released by the creature that had had control of it, for now the motor shot the boat away from the large hummock.

Tommy Lee grasped hold of the tiller and sped away, not the way he had come but around the Nest, and away toward Gavin Pond Farm. He held the rifle across his lap, flung the case of the beer and the men's magazines into the water and never once looked back.

He refused to look back not for fear of what he might see, but for fear of what he *had* seen.

It was not another creature that had stood up from behind one of those two grassy mounds in the center of the Nest, not another gray-green thing with circular staring eyes and a wide lipless mouth and a smooth round head; it had been Elinor Caskey, an old woman, an old woman he knew very well, her face contorted with fear, screaming *Nerita!* And it was Elinor Caskey that Tommy Lee had shot. The bullet had made a small black circle in her bared breast.

When he reached the farm he ran the boat right up through the reeds at the edge of the new pasture and leaped out, stamping through the mud. He groped his way through the strands of the barbed-wire fence at the edge of the pasture and ran all the way back to the house, trailing the barrel of the gun along behind him as he went.

Though the sun that morning had risen in a cloudless sky, and the radio had predicted fair weather for all this day and the next, it was now raining—and raining heavily—by the time Tommy Lee reached the house. His boots and trousers had gotten caked with mud when he had jumped out of the boat, but the rain washed it off and mingled it with the churning mud at the edge of the brick patio. He was sweating with fear and exertion; the rain poured down from the sky and saturated his clothing until he could smell and taste and feel nothing but that. Tommy Lee was scratched and bleeding in a dozen places, but as fast as he bled the rain washed the blood away and drummed it into the earth.

CHAPTER 85

Rain

It rains now, a rain less impressive for its intensity than for its unvarying relentlessness, soaking the sandy yards around the Caskey houses steadily all morning, all afternoon, all evening, and throughout the night. Billy Bronze hears it as he rises from his bed, and it continues throughout his unhappy day and into his unhappy sleep at night, without ever a slackening, or even an increase that could optimistically be interpreted as the darkness before the dawn. The water pours down the roof of all sides of the house, overwhelming the inadequate gutters, falling to the front steps below in a sheet of water heavy enough to smash an umbrella. It cascades into the flower beds that edge the house, digging sharp deep trenches and dislodging bulbs and tubers. It blows against sills and windows, opaquely filling a hundred thousand minute squares in the rusting screens.

The rain is an incessant thunder, inexorable and unnerving, louder than conversation, louder than music, louder than the bus to Mobile careering along the road at a quarter past four. The rain forces Billy to listen for patterns and rhythms that are broken as soon as captured. The sound of rain blots out his thoughts as he rocks in one of the swings on the screened-in porch upstairs; but that—it occurs to him just before giving up trying to think altogether—is just as well, for he does not like to consider that in her room inside, Elinor Caskey lies dying.

How she had been brought home, Billy does not know and never asked. He only knows that late in the afternoon when the rain first began Zaddie knocked on the door of his office and beckoned to him. Zaddie led him to Elinor's bedroom, and there on the bed, still in her drenched clothes, and smelling strongly of the Perdido, lay Elinor Caskey. She tore back the top of her blouse and there he saw, an inch or two over her heart, a small black bullet hole.

"Hold down my legs," she commanded Billy.

Obediently, Billy sat at the foot of the bed and pressed his hands over Elinor's ankles. Zaddie went around to the other side and pressed against Elinor's knees. Billy had no idea what was going on.

"Have you called the doctor?" he asked. "Where is the doctor, Zaddie?"

"No doctor," said Elinor.

"You could die!" Billy protested.

"I *will* die," said Elinor solemnly.

"Who shot you?" Billy asked. "What happened?"

Elinor did not answer. With her head propped on two pillows, she looked down at the wound in her breast. She put her thumb and forefinger together and pushed them inside the small black hole. She hissed through her teeth, and her entire body twisted and bucked. She would have turned over or fallen off the bed, had not Billy and Zaddie so tightly held her legs.

She hissed and screamed—and finally pulled out the bullet.

She lay panting for perhaps two minutes, holding the small lead missile tightly clenched in the palm of her hand. Zaddie wiped her brow with a cloth.

"Tommy Lee did it," said Zaddie.

"Why?" cried Billy in amazement.

"He didn't mean to," whispered Elinor. "It wasn't his fault."

"Elinor, we have—"

"We don't have to do anything," said Elinor. "I'm

168

going to lie here in this bed until I die, and you and Zaddie are going to protect me."

"Protect you from what?" Billy demanded.

There was silence for a long moment.

"Billy," said Elinor after having gathered the strength to speak, "I want you to go and make two telephone calls. Call Tommy Lee and tell him to come into town because I need to speak to him. Call Miriam and tell her that I'm sick and that she should come see me tomorrow. Don't call anybody else. If you call the doctor, I won't see him, and I won't speak to you again. Do you understand?"

Billy nodded, and did just as he was asked.

Tommy Lee came that afternoon and entered the house wet, abashed, guilty—and fearful. Billy took him upstairs to Elinor's room, then waited curiously to see what Elinor would say to him.

But Elinor sent both Billy and Zaddie away, and was alone with Tommy Lee for several minutes. Tommy Lee emerged from that interview more shaken than he had been when he came into the house. He hurried out into the rain, threw himself into his pickup, and barreled off down the flooded road.

"I had to make sure he wouldn't say anything foolish," said Elinor later. "Tommy Lee won't say anything. We don't have to worry about *that*."

Miriam came the next day, as Elinor had requested, and by then Elinor was weaker, but she looked more presentable. Zaddie had bathed her and got her into a nightgown and embroidered bed jacket. The rain continued to pour. Miriam said, "Mama, you look perfectly awful."

"I'm going to die, Miriam."

"Soon, you mean?"

Elinor nodded. "I just wanted you to know that everything is in order—the will, and all the rest of it. Billy knows everything."

"Good," said Miriam. "But I knew that you'd be ready when the time came." She looked at her mother closely. "Are you sure the time has come?" Elinor nodded. "I'm sorry for that," said Miriam briskly. "I really am."

"I think you mean that," said Elinor.

"Are Zaddie and Billy taking care of you?" Miriam asked. "You want me to send Malcolm off for anything?"

"Yes. I want you and Malcolm both to do something for me."

"What's that?"

"One last request, Miriam."

"I won't promise, Mama. But what is it?"

"I don't want you around when I die. I want you and Malcolm to leave town until I'm dead."

"Go away! Mama, I cain't just up and leave the mill—"

"Yes, you can. So do it. Go away until I'm dead. You don't want to be around here anyway, tending to me."

"I wouldn't be tending to you anyway," remarked Miriam. "But where do you want us to go?"

"Go visit Lilah. Go to Houston. If you really have to stay in the area go out and stay with Grace and Lucille. Lord knows they've got plenty of room out there."

"Mama, why don't you want Malcolm and me here?"

"I have my reasons," said Elinor. "And they're good ones. Go away, Miriam. Go away tonight. Or tomorrow. No later than tomorrow."

"Well," said Miriam, "I still haven't promised. I'll have to speak to Malcolm."

"Malcolm will do what you say."

"Mama," said Miriam with some delicacy, "how long do you imagine that Malcolm and I will have to stay away?"

"Miriam," remarked her mother dryly, "what I've left you in my will is going to make up for the inconvenience."

Miriam returned to the house the next morning

with Malcolm and they spoke brief goodbyes to Elinor. The rain kept up.

"You ought to see it out there, Elinor," said Malcolm, shaking his head. "The whole damn yard is about to wash away."

"Where are you two going?"

"Someplace dry," said Miriam.

"Houston for a few days, and then to New York," said Malcolm. "After that, I don't know where."

"Goodbye then," said Elinor. She reached up weakly and took Malcolm's hand and squeezed it. "You be good to Miriam," she said.

Malcolm laughed. "You tell her to be good to *me!*"

Miriam dropped down onto the side of the bed. She took Elinor's other hand and drew it to her breast. She leaned down and kissed Elinor's cheek.

When Miriam drew back, she saw a tear in Elinor's eye.

"Mama," said Miriam, "that's the first time I have ever seen you cry."

Elinor smiled wanly. "It's the first time you ever kissed me."

Miriam stood up. "Goodbye, Mama."

"Goodbye, darling," replied Elinor. "Be good to Malcolm. He probably deserves it."

Zaddie stood at the door downstairs and gave Miriam and Malcolm umbrellas before they stepped out onto the front porch.

"Will you call me?" Miriam quietly asked Zaddie. Zaddie nodded silently. Malcolm led his wife out to their car. It was only a dozen yards away, but by the time they reached it, despite the umbrellas and their haste, they were sodden with rainwater.

Rain has fallen incessantly on Perdido for the past seven days, more than twenty-six inches of precipitation in all. At first, for most people, this persistent inclemency had been nothing more than an excuse to complain—for once with sufficient cause—about the state of the weather. Perdido merchants were certain that customers were being discouraged from driving downtown; and for the farmers, who recently had completed spring planting, it was a disaster. Seedlings were beaten back into the earth or washed down their own furrows to float in thick clots in drainage ditches. Not-yet-sprouted seeds rotted in the earth. With each day the rain continued, the dread of the people in the town increased, for it was no longer simply a question of the nuisance of umbrellas and soggy newspapers, no longer only a matter of reduced retail receipts—it was the threat of another flood.

It did not matter much in fact whether it rained on Perdido or not, but whether there was precipitation in the vast forests northeast and northwest of town was of great concern. Water falling there would wash down the gently sloping land into the Perdido and the Blackwater rivers and would swell those streams from their sources to the junction behind the Perdido town hall. In short, if it continued to rain in the forests where the water and the wetness inconvenienced no one at all, it might very well flood in Perdido.

After the fourth day of rain the weather reports on the Perdido radio station, and even those over the television stations in Pensacola and Mobile, well removed from the danger, had begun to give the heights of the rivers along with daily and cumulative totals of the rainfall. On the seventh day of rain an army engineer was sent down from Fort Rucca to inspect the Perdido levees, for already the water was higher than at any time since 1919.

That engineer drove his jeep to the top of the levee behind the town hall, prodded the earth with a spade, pulled a few blackberry bushes out of the side of the embankment, peered through the rain to the opposite bank of the swollen rivers with his field glasses, and tried to ignore the questions of the mayor, who had insisted on accompanying him on this tour of inspection.

172

From the mayor's house, where he had been invited to lunch, the engineer telephoned Fort Rucca and requested his superior to come down to Perdido that afternoon. In fact, to depart immediately. The mayor and his wife overheard this conversation and were unsettled by it. They became even more worried when the army engineer asked them where a helicopter might set down in the town.

At quarter of two, the army engineer—and each and every one of the town's municipal workers—watched the helicopter descend through the rain into a cleared space in the town hall parking lot. A colonel and two other men, one of them a civilian, emerged. They shook hands with the mayor, then drove off in the first engineer's jeep, peremptorily declining the mayor's offer to tag along.

At half past four, all four men arrived at the mayor's house on Live Oak Street—low land—and informed him that the levee was not safe and might collapse if the water were to reach a level higher than thirty-two feet. At this time the rivers already were at twenty-eight feet. The mayor, as well as his wife and cook, who were listening from the kitchen, were aghast and wanted to know how on earth the levee, which had protected Perdido for more than four decades, could be considered unsafe—it had always been thought of as the most substantial construction in town.

"There are places," the engineer said with a shrug, "where the levee is very weak. Here and there some of the vegetation burned and the levee eroded. There are places that weren't built right in the first place. There's even a break down by the railroad track near the junction. It wasn't kept in repair."

"There's never been enough money," the mayor argued weakly. The engineer shrugged again. "What can we do?" the mayor asked then.

The colonel spoke now, glancing out the window where the rain was falling steadily. He was uncomfortable, for his uniform was wet through and he had

173

an upset stomach from the journey in the helicopter. "I'll send down some men. They'll start arriving tonight and tomorrow. They can try to shore up the levee, filling sandbags, evacuate people if need be, that sort of thing. Can't promise anything, though, can't promise they'll do any good. The only thing I *can* promise is that they'll be here working their goddamn asses off to save this town."

"*Save* it," repeated the mayor in whispered alarm. "What happens," he went on tremulously, "if the levee does break?"

"Well," said one of the other engineers, a younger man who did not understand the niceties of evasion and prevarication, "the water breaks through in one place, and it takes a hell of a lot more of the levee with it. A wall of water rushes in. You'd better have already gotten your people out, because there won't be anyone or anything left in the path of that water. The water would rush in so fast that it would be better to have had no levee at all."

What the man said was accurate, but the colonel and the other engineers glared at him: they had wanted to persuade the mayor, not frighten him, into the advisability of evacuation.

"The hospital..." said the colonel. "Where is the hospital in this town?"

"On high ground," replied the mayor's wife, who entered now with coffee and towels.

"Just as well," said the officer, and no more.

No one in Perdido noticed that Elinor Caskey had not been out of her house in ten days. For ten days the rain had fallen, and Perdido thought of nothing but that. Some children were taken out of the school and sent to their grandparents in places where it wasn't raining and there was no danger of flooding. Those who had beach houses at Gulf Shores or Destin were suddenly overwhelmed with a desire to visit those places, though April was still quite early in the season for the beach. Quietly, at Billy Bronze's

174

suggestion, all the important files of the mill were packed up and taken out to Gavin Pond Farm. It was true that the farmhouse was no more than half a mile from the river, but it was situated on much higher ground than Perdido, and unlikely to be inundated. When that was done, Tommy Lee went to Elinor's house and took away the files in Billy's office, too. And so, day by day, and little by little, Tommy Lee took everything that was important to the Caskeys—including the boxes of jewelry in the bottom of Miriam's dresser—out to Gavin Pond Farm. Grace and Lucille had made so many additions to the house over the years that there was plenty of room for everything to be stored.

After his first interview with Elinor in her bed Tommy Lee did not visit her again; in fact, when he and Escue went to the house to collect some records from Billy's office, Tommy Lee sidled quickly past the door to Elinor's room.

Lucille and Grace did pay a visit to Elinor, a single visit of state, quite formal and brief.

Lucille, looking more and more like Queenie every day, and already surpassing her mother in the matter of girth, stood at the window and looked out. Through the curtain of water that spilled off the roof, Lucille could see the gently twisted narrow trunks of the water oaks that Elinor had planted before she was married to Oscar. She heard their branches creaking beneath the weight of the water, and once after a sodden *crack,* she saw a large branch, leafless and rotten, fall from the very top of the tree to the ground, where it landed with a loud splash in the sheet of shallow water that covered the yard. Lucille did not want to look at Elinor. Tommy Lee had told them that Elinor was dying.

Grace had pulled a chair up close to the side of the bed.

"Tommy Lee says you are dying," said Grace. "Did he know what he was talking about?"

Elinor nodded solemnly. "I am dying," she said.

"Are you in pain?" Grace asked.

"Yes," said Elinor.

"Is there anything Lucille and I can do?"

"No," said Elinor. "One thing," she amended.

"What?" said Lucille, turning with alacrity. She felt helpless, and was glad to hear there was *something* to be done for Elinor.

Elinor spoke softly, but with deliberation. "Tell Tommy Lee that it was not his fault."

Grace and Lucille exchanged glances.

"Does he think it was?" asked Grace. When Elinor nodded, Grace said, "What is wrong with you, Elinor?"

Elinor shook her head. "Just make sure Tommy Lee knows that it wasn't his fault."

Lucille was about to speak, but Grace said quickly and with finality, "We will. It wasn't his fault," she repeated, as if to get the message straight.

"You're tired," said Lucille solicitously. "We'll come back tomorrow."

"No," said Elinor. "Say goodbye now."

"You have to let us come back!" exclaimed Lucille.

"Stay out at the farm," said Elinor. "Don't come back into town."

"Why not?" asked Grace.

"Because the levee is going to break," said Elinor. "And I don't want you to get caught."

Lucille involuntarily glanced out of the window at the kudzu-covered embankment beyond the water oaks. "It's not gone break, Elinor!"

"Are you sure?" said Grace to Elinor, ignoring Lucille's wishful thinking. Elinor nodded. "Then you ought to let us take you out to the farm where you'll be safe. Lucille, start packing Elinor a bag."

"No," said Elinor. "I'm staying here."

"And get washed away?" Lucille demanded.

Elinor only smiled.

"What about Billy and Zaddie?" asked Grace. "What happens to them if the levee breaks? You ought to let them bring you out to the farm. We've got so much room!"

"I'm tired," said Elinor weakly. "Say goodbye to me and go back out to the farm. You'll be safe there."

Lucille and Grace stood at the side of the bed holding hands.

"I cain't say goodbye!" exclaimed Lucille. "Oh, Elinor, don't make me say goodbye!"

"Goodbye, Lucille. Queenie was very proud of you. We've all been proud of you."

Lucille turned away and began to weep softly.

"Goodbye, Elinor," said Grace.

"Open that top drawer," said Elinor. "And take out the box that's right at the front."

Grace did so; inside the box were Elinor's black pearls.

"James gave those to Genevieve," said Elinor. "They should come to you now."

"No," said Grace. "I couldn't take them."

"Mary-Love got all of Genevieve's other jewelry, and Miriam has it now. Miriam's not likely to give any of it up, so take the pearls, Grace."

"I'll wait," she said softly.

"You can't wait. When I die, I'm not leaving anything behind." Elinor glanced around the room and smiled. "Not a thing. If you don't take them now, those pearls will be lost forever, and I'd hate to think of that happening."

Grace nodded and put the box of pearls into her purse.

"You're the only one left who was alive when I came to Perdido," said Elinor. "It's hard to believe they're all dead."

"I remember," said Grace. "I remember sitting on your knee out at Miz Driver's church. I remember when you came to live with Daddy and me."

"A long time ago. You were such a little girl back then—a prissy little girl." Elinor laughed softly.

"I loved you very much, Elinor," said Grace simply. "I always have. I do now."

"It hurts me to say goodbye," said Elinor. "To you especially."

Grace leaned over the bed and quickly embraced Elinor. Then she stood up, wiped her eyes, and walked out of the room. Lucille quickly followed.

"Goodbye! Goodbye!" Elinor called weakly after them until her voice was lost to them beneath the beating of the rain against the windows of the house.

On the eleventh day of rain, the U.S. Army Corps of Engineers officially advised all residents of Perdido to evacuate the town and move to higher ground. Many had already done so, and those who had stubbornly stayed, trusting the levee and their own good luck, gave second thoughts to the advisability of remaining in a town that might very soon be washed away. The foolhardily curious climbed the levee, and were astonished at the height of the water. The grove of live oaks north of the junction was now no more than a black field of water punctuated by monumental green domes. The forests to the northwest of Perdido were flooded, and no logging could be done within ten miles of the town. To the northeast, the swamp in which the Blackwater River had its source had long since overflowed its bounds and the road between Perdido and Atmore was closed. To the south of town, the Perdido was more than twice its usual width; shrubs and small trees along its banks were drowned, and a number of even the biggest trees had been uprooted by the pressure of the flowing black water.

The National Guard had been in town for three days, sandbagging the levee, and knocking on the doors of every house to make certain that the residents were alert to the danger. Downtown shops closed, and trucks were loaded with merchandise to be stored temporarily on high ground. The Caskey mill shut down under orders from Miriam—now in New York City—and most of the workers left town. All the lumber and other wood products that had been warehoused in the vicinity were trucked down to Bay Minette, not because Bay Minette was convenient, but because the road to the southwest was the only one that seemed safe against flooding. A siren was installed in the room beneath the clocks in the town hall, and its sounding was to be warning that the levee had broken.

The installation of that siren convinced the doubting Thomases of Perdido, as nothing else had before, that the town lay in great danger. The National Guard, these people considered, was always doing something or other to keep their men busy, and they might as well fill sandbags as anything else. The U.S. Army Corps of Engineers was always looking for an excuse to throw its weight around and declare this and that construction unsafe and dangerous. The mayor always grabbed any opportunity to appear important and capable. The sandbags, the engineers' warnings, and the mayor's frenzied busyness could be shrugged off, but that siren in the room beneath the town hall clocks could not be. The rivers were at thirty-one feet, and everyone—or almost everyone—left town.

The patients in the Perdido hospital had all been transferred to Bay Minette or Mobile. Because the hospital was on high ground, the National Guard now slept in its beds at night. They were confident that the town had been completely evacuated.

The supports for the bridge that crossed from downtown to Baptist Bottom had been weakened by the water, and on the evening of the twelfth day of rain the bridge came loose. The underpinnings of the Baptist Bottom side went first, and with terrible creakings and snappings the bridge swung southward along the line of the current. Two unlucky National Guardsmen were walking across the bridge at the time, their jeep having stalled in a huge puddle in Baptist Bottom. They ran and jumped for the levee just as the bridge was knocked completely loose. One of them made it, but the other slipped in the mud of the levee and slid into the water. He caught, for a moment, onto a twisted piling of the bridge that remained. His hands and arms were torn as he attempted to climb out of the reach of the rushing water. The noise made by the bridge as it was wracked and crumbled was deafening; the incessant rain out of the black sky was blinding. The National Guardsman who had gained the safety of the levee heard his friend scream from his precarious perch on that tilted piling, and he *thought* he saw him dragged under the water—by two long arms that ended in flat webbed hands.

Billy Bronze sat in the dark on the upstairs screened-in porch on the evening of the twelfth day of rain. The screens were opaque with rainwater. Rainwater splashed on the half-railing all around the porch. Rainwater still poured in a steady sheet from the eaves of the house.

He sat in the dark, for at night now he and Zaddie did not turn on any lights except in Elinor's room, and there the curtains were tightly drawn. The National Guard had been there three days ago, and Billy had promised them that he would go away within the hour. Zaddie had gone around, locking up, drawing the curtains, just as if they had intended to leave. Elinor would not go, and Zaddie and Billy had no intention of abandoning her.

It occurred to him now, almost for the first time, that this loyalty might mean his own death, and Zaddie's. If the levee behind the house broke, then they and the house were sure to be swept away. He and Zaddie would be drowned or crushed in the catastrophe.

He pondered this for some time, not out of fear, but as a way to pass the time. It somehow did not seem so much for Elinor to ask; he certainly had no intention of remonstrating with her on the matter. Even if she did die before the levee broke—even if she were dead *now,* he thought, glancing over his

180

shoulder—he and Zaddie would probably stay on with the corpse until the rains subsided and the rivers receded. Or until the river broke through the levee. It somehow wouldn't be right to carry Elinor's body out through the rain.

He continued to sit and rock slowly in the swing, and though it grew late, he did not listen for the slow and surreptitious footsteps to come up the stairs on a visit to Elinor. Frances and Nerita—he thought of those visitors by name now—had stayed away since Elinor had appeared with the bullet hole in her breast. They had not come since the day that the rain began its assault on Perdido.

He rose and went inside. There was something a little frightening about being in a house that was supposed to be empty, in a town that had been evacuated, knowing that the siren, if and when it blew, would blow to warn them alone, they who would not heed its warning. Billy felt himself an intruder in that dark silent house. Only Elinor's bedroom, with a single lamp burning with pine-scented oil—and burning always, throughout the black night and the dark, rain-sodden days—seemed of any comfort to him at all. And that room housed a dying old woman.

He was turning the knob on the door to Elinor's sitting room when he thought he heard a noise at the far end of the hallway, something that wasn't rain, that wasn't the creaking of furniture, something that was as surreptitious as those footsteps of Frances's had once been. Billy did not pause, but pushed open the door of the sitting room and went inside. Long accustomed to the darkness, he found the line of light around the door into Elinor's bedroom blinding. He stood a few moments until his eyes had adjusted, and then went in.

Thin and pale and looking ancient with all her makeup long washed off, her eyes closed, and her feeble hands curled palms up atop the neatly folded covers, Elinor Caskey lay in the center of the bed. She was the very picture of a dying woman, like an

181

old engraving—sentimental and pretty—of how such a thing *ought* to be done. Zaddie lay sleeping on a cot at the side of the bed; she stirred drowsily as Billy entered. She and Billy did not leave Elinor alone for a minute.

Elinor slowly opened her eyes and, seeing Billy, smiled.

"How are you?" he asked quietly.

"Poor Billy," she said. "You won't have much longer to wait."

Billy shrugged, and went and sat on the edge of the bed. Elinor hadn't the strength to move her hands, but he saw them trembling there, and grasped them both.

"Tonight," Elinor said, "you stay with me—you and Zaddie, both of you, all night long, you hear?"

Billy's eyebrows creased, but he did not argue. If he had accepted her refusal to see a doctor or enter the hospital, was he going to balk at such a minor point as this?

"Zaddie," said Elinor. "Wake up."

Though Elinor's voice was scarcely a whisper, Zaddie instantly roused herself. "Ma'am?"

"Go downstairs and fix some food for you and Billy. Don't worry about the lights. Nobody's going to be out tonight. Then bring it back up here. Go now, and don't dawdle."

Zaddie did just as she was told. When she had gone, Elinor said to Billy, "Get out the box of keys that's in the second drawer of the bureau. Go through them and find the ones that fit the sitting room door and the door of this room." She closed her eyes then, as if the effort to say even that much had cost her a lot.

The sitting room door had never been locked before. Neither had the door of this bedroom. Billy knew that. He went through a dozen keys before he found the two that turned the tumblers in the locks. He then waited at the door of the sitting room for Zaddie to return. In a few moments she came up the stairs bearing a tray with sandwiches and beer. He opened the door for her, and then whispered, "I'm just going to get my glasses. I'll be right back."

He went across the hall to his own room, fumbled for the right case on top of the dresser, tried to think if there was anything else he might need but could think of nothing. Then he was startled to hear, above the noise of the rain, two voices. They came from inside the house and they were not those of Elinor and Zaddie; they were of a woman and a child, and they came from the front room.

Slipping his glasses into the pocket of his shirt, without thinking he went to the door to the linen closet. He quietly turned the handle and pulled it slowly open. That closed windowless corridor was pitch dark at first, but then Billy could see that the door at its opposite end was slowly being opened. There in the dim light that suffused the front room, he could see an old woman with her hand on the knob. Billy did not recognize her. Next to her was a child whom he did not recognize either. The old woman gave a little smile, pointed at Billy, then pushed the boy into the corridor. The boy, holding out his hands before him, stumbled down between the shelves of sheets and towels toward Billy.

Billy slammed the door shut, and rushed out of his room and across the hallway, not even glancing back. He stumbled into the sitting room and slammed the door closed. He pulled what he thought was the right key from his pocket and slipped it quickly into the lock. The key did not turn. He jerked it out, and tried a second key. This one did turn, but even before Billy had taken his hand away, he saw the knob of the door turning.

"Go away," he whispered.

He stepped quickly into Elinor's bedroom, blinded by the light once more. He carefully shut the door, and locked it also.

Elinor slowly opened her eyes and looked at him

183

with such profound knowing that he asked automatically, "Who were they?"

"Mary-Love," said Elinor.

"Oscar's mother? She was dead before—" He abruptly ceased to argue. "And the boy?"

"His name is John Robert DeBordenave. He used to live in the house beyond James's."

"When?" asked Billy.

"A long time ago. Right, Zaddie?" said Elinor with a smile. "You remember John Robert? When you and Grace were little and Mary-Love tried to make Grace play with him instead of you?"

Zaddie said to Billy, "John Robert was lacking in the head," as if that explained why Zaddie was old and John Robert still looked no more than ten.

"Is that why we're locking the door?" Billy asked.

Elinor closed her eyes, as if she didn't intend to waste her strength responding to questions with answers that were obvious.

"What do we do now?" Billy asked.

"Now?" echoed Elinor. "Now we wait."

Zaddie and Billy sat with Elinor long into that night. Billy moved his chair from near the door to a place near the window. When he sat near the door, he could hear the distant relentless scraping outside the sitting room door. When he was near the window he could hear nothing but the rain.

As Elinor grew weaker, the rain seemed to fall harder. So Zaddie and Billy sat, silent and watching, as Elinor Caskey moved slowly toward death. They waited for that death to come, or for the rain to stop, or for the siren's wail across the town through the sound of the falling water—though it might be, both Zaddie and Billy knew, that the water would arrive without any warning at all.

Suddenly there was a loud crash in the next room, and before Billy and Zaddie even had time to realize that it had been the sound of the sitting room door being broken open, they saw the knob on the bed-

184

room door turn, first slowly, then frantically. When that was of no avail, the scratching and low pounding began closer to hand, right on the other side of the door.

Billy and Zaddie glanced at one another, and then at Elinor.

Her eyes were open now, and her face was serene. "Give me your hands," she whispered.

On her left was Zaddie, and Zaddie took Elinor's hand. On her right was Billy Bronze, and Billy took her other hand.

Billy and Zaddie leaned close to hear her words. The rain beat riotously against the windows. There was pounding against the door of the bedroom, incessant and now crazed sounding.

"Goodbye, Billy. You became my son."

Billy said nothing, but squeezed Elinor's unresponsive hand tighter.

"Goodbye, Zaddie. We were good to each other, weren't we?"

"Yes, ma'am," replied Zaddie. "We sure were."

Thunder now came, and the rain beat against the house, and in thunder the blows against the bedroom door were redoubled, and over the top of it all came two screams: one of frustration just beyond the shaking bedroom door, and one all over the town itself as the siren in the room beneath the town hall clocks began to wail. The levee had burst.

The door of the bedroom flew open, and Zaddie and Billy had one glimpse there of Mary-Love and John Robert, pale, white, and dead.

Elinor closed her eyes. "Goodbye," she whispered then, without hurry and without fear, and was gone.

The levee split in two places at once. The western side of the Perdido, just where the bridge had been, had always been a weak spot. The bridge, in tearing itself away, had taken with it many tons of hard-packed clay, and flowing water in patient and tenacious eddies had eaten away much more over the

185

past few hours. Deeper and deeper inroads had been made, until at last, precisely at half past three in the morning, the water of the combined Perdido and Blackwater rivers broke through entirely. In a matter of moments, the line of stores along the eastern side of Palafox Street was shoved right across the street into the line of stores opposite. In another minute everything was splinters and shards of glass and mounds of paper, all blackened with water. The livelihoods of tradesmen were transformed in an instant into a battering ram of debris which, in a dozen different directions at once, hurled itself against the rest of the town. The flood swept swiftly along, tearing up streets, telephone poles, trees, and houses. Whole buildings were smashed into atoms of timber no larger than toothpicks. Others simply had their second stories sheared off, and whole furnished rooms coasted off on the surface of the inexorable black tide until they smashed against a tree or some other building, and became themselves instruments of destruction.

On the eastern side of the town, the levee was sundered just behind the Caskey mill, a hundred yards or so before the Blackwater reached the junction. That smaller river had less force than the Perdido below the junction, but the damage it did was complete. The Caskey warehouses, outbuildings, offices, trucks, and oil storage facilities were first inundated, then either shivered to bits or else lifted up and carried into Baptist Bottom where, one by one, as if God had possessed a municipal map and were checking off the meager dwellings in malign sequence, the houses of Baptist Bottom and all the belongings of the poor people who had lived there were crushed beneath tons of black water and debris. Several large oil tanks had been broken open, and now the surface of the flood was covered with a lugubrious sheen.

And still the rain cascaded down upon the scene of destruction.

The National Guardsmen stationed on the roof of the hospital peered through their field glasses. In the blackness they had seen nothing, and their first indication that the levees had burst had been the explosive noise of the water suddenly surging into the town. That was when the siren was sounded, but the siren blew for no more than a few seconds before all the power in the town was lost. Without further heralding, the water set about to wipe Perdido from the face of the earth.

The levee behind the Caskey houses held, but it made little difference. Before the levee had burst downtown, water had begun to spill over the top of the embankment. Black water tumbled through the kudzu vines and covered the yards with a sheet of water that grew higher by the minute. When the levee finally did cave in downtown, the water increased even more rapidly, but because a small residential hill and several thick stands of trees lay between the Caskey houses and the major break, the debris was kept at bay. Only the water came, lapping in waves against the foundations of Elinor's house, then breaking against the first-floor windows, smashing in the stained glass in the front parlor, spilling into the rooms, swirling about under the legs of the furniture, surging into the hearths and gouging out all the accumulated years of ashes and soot. Water rose through the floorboards into all the rooms, overturning delicate furniture, smashing small objects against the walls, pushing debris from room to room. Water crept up the stairs to the second floor. And all this in blackness, and with not as much noise as the continuing crashing of the rain outside the house.

But the rain was slackening.

Upstairs, Elinor Caskey lay dead.

At the moment of her death, the terrible apparitions in the doorway—Mary-Love and John Robert—had simply disappeared. They were no longer there. The broken, battered door swung shut of its own accord. Zaddie sat on the edge of the bed, still holding Elinor's hand. Billy went to the door and opened it. He looked out and saw nothing. He went through the sitting room and into the hallway. What he heard was the water sloshing about downstairs; he leaned over the banister and looked down. He saw black water on the lower stairs. It was already three feet deep on the first floor and still rising.

He returned to Elinor's bedroom and looked out the window. The water was about eight feet deep in the yard. He could see it spilling over the top of the levee.

He walked over to the bed and took dead Elinor's other hand.

"I don't expect we can get away, Zaddie," he said.

Zaddie shook her head, and said with proud solemnity, "Miss Elinor say to me, long time ago, 'Zaddie, that levee gone hold up till I die, and then that water gone wash this town away.'"

They sat and they waited; gradually the rain tapered off. The effect of so much silence was eerie to Billy and Zaddie, much eerier than the fact that they were sitting and holding the hands of a dead woman, much eerier than the sounds they heard from below of the furniture knocking against the walls and ceilings of the first-floor rooms.

After a time, Zaddie looked down at the floor and lifted her feet experimentally. The carpet was sodden.

"Starting to come through," she remarked.

Billy only nodded; he had already seen that.

Zaddie and Billy waited with infinite patience, not once thinking of rescue, or attempting to get away. Now and then Billy turned to the window and glanced to see if the dawn was near, but the sky remained absolutely black. It was still covered with clouds, but the clouds now merely scudded past, and dropped no more rain.

Both Zaddie and Billy were lost in their own

thoughts; Elinor's hands grew cold in theirs. Finally, dawn began slowly to creep in upon them. The water was more than a foot deep in the room, and Zaddie and Billy had pulled up their feet into their chairs. Small objects floated in from the hallway like tiny curious animals and, after abiding awhile, floated back out again. As the dawn became strong, the two weary people were roused by a bumping sound that was louder than the others.

"What was that?" Zaddie said quickly.

Billy shook his head. "Something knocking against the side of the house, that's all. I imagine pretty much everything in this town is floating around. I'm surprised we haven't had any telephone poles poke through the window."

The knock was repeated, twice in rapid succession. It sounded insistent.

Billy slowly let go of Elinor's hand, and placed it on her breast. He went to the window and looked out, blinking against the light.

"What is it?" Zaddie asked.

"A boat," said Billy calmly. "Somebody has tied a boat to this window." He turned back to Zaddie. "Come on, Zaddie. It's time for us to go."

"Cain't leave Miss Elinor," said Zaddie.

"Yes, we can," said Billy. He waded across the room and out through the sitting room into the hallway. "Frances!" he called, not with questioning or timidity, but with complete confidence that she was there. No answer came, but Billy went on, "Frances, Zaddie and I are going on now. You take care of Elinor, will you?"

Without waiting for a reply, he went back into the bedroom. Zaddie was leaning over the bed, pressing her cheek against Elinor's, cold and wasted.

"I'm ready, Mr. Billy," she said.

Billy was at the window. He reached out, pulled the boat nearer, and with some awkwardness, climbed into it. He grasped hold of the sill and tried to hold

189

the boat steady while Zaddie, with much greater awkwardness, somehow got into it.

Immediately, Billy untied the boat and began to row away from the house. Zaddie, seated in the stern, turned to look back, but Billy said, "No. Don't." But his own gaze never moved from the open window through which they had climbed. And what he saw there through that window made him weep as he paddled away.

So through the dawn of that morning that broke on the destruction of Perdido, Billy Bronze and Zaddie Sapp rowed slowly toward high ground.

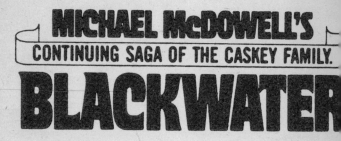